Poor Little Poor Girl

Book 1

Based on true stories;

Inspired by real-life events

Christopher "Link" Wynn

COPYRIGHT

First Edition

Library of Congress Control Number: 2025928275 |

ISBN (Paperback): 979-8-9942005-0-6 // ISBN (eBook): 979-8-9942005-1-3 //

ISBN (Audiobook): 979-8-9942005-4-4 // ISBN (Hardcover): 979-8-1968656-7-1 //

Poor Little Poor Girl — Book 1

Published by

Wynning Entertainment Publishing

email: wynningentertainment33@gmail.com

United States of America

Printed in the United States of America

Publisher's Cataloging-in-Publication
Provided by Cassidy Cataloguing Services, Inc.

Names: Wynn, Christopher (Link), author.

Title: Poor little poor girl. Book 1 / Christopher "Link" Wynn.

Description: First edition. | [Harrisburg, North Carolina] : Wynning Entertainment Publishing, [2026] | "Based on true stories; inspired by real-life events."

Identifiers: LCCN: 2025928275 | ISBN: 9798994200506 (paperback) | 9798196865671 (hardcover) 9798994200513 (eBook) | 9798994200544 (audiobook)

Subjects: LCSH: Child trafficking victims. | Human trafficking victims. | Resilience (Personality trait) | Courage. | Human trafficking. | Human trafficking--Prevention. | International crimes. | Suspense fiction. | LCGFT: Fiction. | Thrillers (Fiction) | Action and adventure fiction. | Detective and mystery fiction. | BISAC: FICTION / Thrillers / Suspense. | FICTION / Action & Adventure. | FICTION / Mystery & Detective / International Crime & Mystery.

Classification: LCC: PS3623.Y646 P66 Bk.1 2026 | DDC: 813/.6--dc23

CONTENT WARNING

This book contains depictions of human trafficking, physical and psychological violence, trauma, and exploitation. These themes may be distressing for some readers. Reader discretion is advised.

PROLOGUE

This is not merely a story of survival, nor is it simply a chronicle of tragedy. It is a testament to resilience, to courage, and to the unyielding human spirit. It is the story of Thalía Salazar, a girl taken from innocence and forced into a world of unimaginable darkness, who refused to let that darkness define her.

Her journey is one of pain and fury, of endurance sharpened into resolve. It is a story that confronts the deepest shadows of humanity: the cruelty that exploits, the systems that fail, and the silence that allows harm to persist. Yet it is also a story of hope—fragile, hard-won, and powerful—of love that refuses to disappear, and of justice pursued at great cost.

From the beginning, Thalía's life was shaped by hardship. But she did not remain a victim. She fought not only to reclaim herself, but to give voice to those who were never given the chance to speak. Through her story, we are asked to bear witness to the realities of trafficking, to the moral complexities of survival and vengeance, and to the question of what justice truly means when innocence has been stolen.

Intertwined with hers is the story of Marco Salazar, her cousin. His love, loyalty, and determination illuminate the lengths one will go to protect family, to honor the fallen, and to confront evil when turning away is no longer an option. Together, their paths are marked by loss and defiance, grief and action, culminating in a legacy that reaches beyond their own lives.

Many of the events depicted in this book are inspired by real-world experiences and truths. They are portrayed with intensity and unflinching honesty, not to shock or sensationalize, but to illuminate what so often remains hidden. This story exists to acknowledge realities that are uncomfortable, painful, and necessary to confront.

If you choose to walk these pages, may you recognize the power of a single voice, a single act, a single life to ignite change. May you feel the heartbreak and the hope, the rage and the resolve. And may this story serve as a reminder that even in the darkest night, courage can endure—and that no spark, once lit, is ever truly extinguished.

Table of Contents

Introduction

The year was 1985.

In a forgotten corner of Honduras, buried beneath poverty and hardship, lived two children whose bond was stronger than blood. **Thalía** and **Marco**, cousins by birth but siblings at heart, were born into a world that gave them little and demanded much. Their parents struggled to put food on the table, teaching them responsibility and respect, while shielding them as best they could from the harshness that surrounded them.

Theirs was a community scarred by hunger, drugs, and crime. In a land where justice could be bought, and politicians ruled with greed while turning their backs on the poor, survival itself was a daily battle. Disease spread quickly where hospitals were scarce, and the dark shadow of human-trafficking grew heavier with every passing year, preying on the most vulnerable.

Yet within this world of despair, Thalía (8 years old) and Marco (6 years old) carried something rare, something that made them both stand out and set apart. Each was born with a rare condition called heterochromia, in which the iris of the eyes are two different colors. One eye a striking light gray, the other a deep hazel brown. To their village, it was a curiosity. To other children, it was something to mock. Their differences became their burden, often at times drawing whispers, stares, and ridicule.

Though the family remained bound to poverty, **Pablo,** Thalía's father began to see beyond their circumstances. He spoke often of a new life, a future far from the corruption and suffering of Honduras. He dreamed of the United States, a place he believed held the promise of safety, dignity, and opportunity for his children.

And so, while hardship still pressed in on every side, Thalía and Marco grew up with that dream whispered into their ears: that one day they would rise above the chains of poverty, that one day they would escape, and that one day they would live a life where hope outshined despair. Until one day... everything changed.

CHAPTER 1

Shadows Over the Village

Night fell heavy over the village, but there was no peace in its darkness. Honduras 1985, the war for power was not fought on distant battlefields, it was waged in the dirt streets of forgotten towns, where the poor became collateral in the struggle of mercenaries and drug lords.

It began with the roar of trucks and the crackle of gunfire tearing through the silence. Shadows stormed into the village, faces masked, machine guns raised. Mercenaries kicked in doors with brute force, dragging men from their homes, shouting threats that rattled the air.

Some were rivals in the drug trade, targets marked for death.

But others were simply fathers, brothers, or bystanders who had the misfortune of standing in the path of violence.

The night became a symphony of chaos: screams, shattering wood, and the relentless bursts of gunfire echoing against the tin roofs. Families cowered in corners, clutching one another as the mercenaries unleashed their fury. Women wept silently, praying their homes would be spared. Children trembled, learning far too young the sound of death.

By dawn, the streets told the story. Bodies lay where they had fallen, blood soaking into the soil of a village already starved of hope. Mothers wailed over their sons. Survivors staggered from hiding places, their faces hollow with shock. What had once been a fragile place of survival was now scarred by terror.

But even in the face of brutality, the people endured. For those who lived through the night, the rising sun was not a promise of peace, but a reminder that they were still alive, that somehow, they had made it through the storm of relentlessness terror.

And among them were two children, cousins bound by more than family ties, who would grow up beneath these shadows. Thalía and Marco did not yet understand the weight of what they had witnessed, but their story, the story of rising above the cruelty of this world was only beginning.

CHAPTER 2

The Set-Up

The village lay in silence, as if the earth itself was holding its breath. Smoke still lingered from the chaos of the night before, curling in the pale morning light. No one dared to move, not even to whisper. Behind shuttered windows and broken doors, the villagers prayed the mercenaries had gone on to their next conquest.

The gunfire had finally ceased, a few of the braver souls began to emerge from the shadows. Slowly, cautiously, they stepped into the open, their eyes scanning the lifeless streets for any sign of movement. They were not searching for safety, they were searching for their loved ones, clinging to the fragile hope that someone, anyone, might still be alive.

Among them was **Pablo**, clutching the hand of his wife, **Consuela**. They had a daughter **Thalía**, whose wide frightened eyes missed nothing. Across the courtyard lived Consuela's sister, **Jessica**, along with her husband **Fredo** and their young son **Marco**. Consuela's heart pounded in her chest as the memory of the mercenaries kicking down her sister Jessica's door replayed in her mind.

(her voice trembling) "They went in there," she whispered frantically to Pablo. "I saw them with my own eyes, Pablo. You must go check on them, please!"

Pablo placed a firm hand on her shoulder, his lips rolled under and pressed tight. "Not yet. It's not safe. Give it time. If they're alive, they're hiding… and if I go now, I'll lead death straight to them!"

But Consuela's fear was stronger than his reason. Her breath came in shallow bursts, panic rising with each second of silence. Not thinking rationally, she says. "I can't just sit here. If you won't go, then I swear to you, I will."

Pablo's heart sank. He knew his wife well enough to understand her resolve. Nothing he said could hold her back. Before he could stop her, Consuela broke free of his grip, darting across the courtyard. Not even noticing she had lost one of her shoes, her bare foot slapped against the dirt as she ran, her body driven by a single desperate need: to see her sister alive.

"Consuela!" Pablo hissed, grabbing Thalía by the hand and into his arms, as he ran after her. He tried to steady her pace, pulling her close, urging her to move with caution rather than reckless speed. But Consuela was beyond reason, her love for her sister outweighed every fear.

When they reached Jessica's home, relief flooded them. Jessica and her family were there, alive, pressed against the doorway with tears of joy. The sisters embraced tightly, clinging to one another as though their reunion could banish the horrors of the night. For a brief, fragile moment, there was laughter, soft, broken, but real.

But joy has a way of drawing shadows.

From behind the crumbling wall, a figure emerged. He was tall, his presence commanding, and on his head wearing a black beret adorned with a nickel-plated wolf emblem. He was *El Lobo "The Wolf"*, a name that had preceded him through the region long before his arrival. A name whispered in terror throughout the villages. A former military colonel turned rogue. The Wolf; Cunning, Ruthless, a predator who never left survivors.

At his side stood a female mercenary, her cold eyes gleaming with malice. They had heard the laughter. They had heard the reunion. And now, they stepped into view, hatred twisting their faces as their weapons hung ready.

The moment of joy evaporated in an instant.

The Wolf had found them.

Poor Little Poor Girl

CHAPTER 3

Pleas in the Dusty-Dawn

The air was still heavy and thick with the smoke from extinguished fires. The stench of blood, gunpowder and despair lingered. Silence hung, broken only by the soft whimpers of frightened children.

Under the pale daylight, Pablo fell to his knees before the mercenaries, his trembling hands raised in surrender. His voice cracked with desperation, but still, he begged.

"Please," he choked, his words trembling with fear and hope alike. "We are only poor villagers. We have nothing, nothing to do with the drugs, nothing at all to do with this war. Spare us. We'll do anything you ask. Just… let us live."

Behind him, Consuela and Jessica clutched their children close, their arms wrapped around them like fragile shields. Their cries joined Pablo's, desperate echoes that pierced the night.

"We'll do anything," Consuela pleaded, her voice breaking. "Please don't hurt us!"

The female mercenary shifted, her cold eyes flicking to El Lobo at her side. Her voice was calm, almost calculating.

"Maybe we could use them. No one would suspect a family like this. They could smuggle for us, and carry our shipments across borders. They might be useful."

But El Lobo "the Wolf" snarled in contempt. His face caught the moonlight as his lip curled with hatred.

"No," he spat, each word dripping venom. "They're weak. Cowards. They'd betray us the first chance they get. Besides, I never leave any witnesses, you know that."

His gaze swept over the huddled family like a predator surveying prey. Then, with the cold finality of death itself, he barked the order: "Kill them, now!"

For the briefest moment, hesitation flickered in the woman's eyes. Her finger hovered over the trigger, caught between mercy and obedience. But it was fleeting. With regret, she raised her weapon. El Lobo mirrored her, his own machine gun steady, his eyes merciless.

The room erupted in thunder.

Gunfire shattered the stillness, a deafening roar of destruction. Pablo was struck first, his body convulsed as bullets tore through him, blood blooming across his chest before pooling beneath him. The women screamed, but their cries were cut short as Consuela, Jessica, and their husbands fell lifeless, collapsing where they stood.

Thalía and Marco stood frozen in horror, clutching each other so tightly their knuckles turned white. Their wide eyes stared at the bodies of their parents, their minds unable to comprehend the nightmare before them. Fear kept their voices locked in their throats.

And still, Pablo (Thalía,'s Father) clung to life. With trembling hands, his body wracked in pain, he lifted the palm of his hand to the mercenaries. His words were faint, no stronger than a dying breath.

"Please... the children. Don't... don't hurt the children. They're innocent. They're just little ones..."

El Lobo was not satisfied. He stepped forward and fired one last shot into Pablo's body.

"Now he's done," he muttered, his lips curling into a cruel smile.

Pablo's chest rose and fell in shallow gasps, until finally it stopped. His body fell still, his spirit leaving him behind.

The female mercenary flinched at the unnecessary act, a shadow of unease crossing her face. But she quickly hid it, her voice sharp.

"That's enough. Let's go. They're as good as dead anyways."

El Lobo turned, his eyes narrowing at the children. "What don't you understand about no survivors?"

Slowly, deliberately, he raised his weapon one last time, aiming at Thalía! His finger tightened around the trigger.

Click!

The sound echoed hollow in the night. Empty.

El Lobo cursed under his breath, glaring at his weapon. Frustration burned across his face. The woman's voice cut through the silence.

"Leave it. They won't last. They're walking ghosts now. The world will finish what we didn't."

El Lobo's teeth clenched, but after a long, seething pause, he lowered his gun. His eyes lingered on the children, two trembling souls framed by blood and ruin. He turned and stalked into the darkness, the woman followed, her gaze flickering back once more before she too disappeared.

And then there was silence.

Thalía stood frozen, her small hand gripping Marco's so tightly it hurt. Around them lay the broken bodies of their parents, the air thick with smoke and sorrow. Tears burned in her eyes, but she refused to let them fall, until she realized the truth.

Her father had saved her. That final plea, that final breath, that final bullet… it was supposed to be for her.

The dam within her broke. Silent tears streamed down her face as she held Marco into her arms, pressing his trembling head against her chest. He was only six. He didn't understand the full weight of what they had lost, but he felt it, the emptiness, the fear, the unbearable silence of being alone.

Two fragile children, left behind in a broken world.

But in that moment, amidst the ruin and the ashes, something inside Thalía hardened. She understood that survival had a price. And though they were small, though they were powerless, their story was not over.

Not yet.

CHAPTER 4

The Rescue

For what felt like an eternity, Thalía and Marco did not move. Their bare feet stood planted in a pool of blood that was no longer warm. The silence pressed in around them, broken only by the faint crackle of burning wood somewhere in the distance.

They clung to each other, paralyzed by fear. Their world, everything they had known was gone, erased in the span of a night. Childhood had ended here, in this room of shadows and death.

An hour passed. Perhaps more. Time had no meaning anymore. The children didn't speak. They barely breathed. The weight of despair held them still as statues, as though any movement might summon the mercenaries back from the dark.

And then, footsteps...

At first, the children flinched, thinking El Lobo had returned to finish what he started. But the sound was different. Softer. Familiar. Emerging from the darkness came five villagers, three men and two women, faces grim, eyes red with grief. They froze when they entered the room, the devastation before them sinking into their hearts like a blade.

One of the women gasped, her hand flying to her mouth. The men lowered their heads in silence. They all knew these families.

They had shared meals, shared laughter, shared struggles. And now, nothing remained but bodies and two trembling children.

Without hesitation, the villagers rushed forward. One woman wrapped her arms around Thalía, pulling her close, rocking her as though she were her own child. Another man crouched before Marco, his large calloused hand resting gently on the boy's shoulder.

"You're safe now," he whispered, though his voice trembled with the lie. "You're safe."

The children were lifted from the blood-soaked floor and carried out into the open air. They felt the comfort of arms around them, the warmth of voices trying to soothe their terror. These villagers had families of their own, mouths already hungry, hearts already burdened, but to leave the children alone would be unforgivable. They would take them in, whatever the cost.

As the night deepened, the survivors turned to the grim task of tending to the dead. Bodies were laid side by side, carefully and reverently. Before burial, a ritual was observed, one passed down through generations of sorrow.

Thalía watched through tear-filled eyes as they removed the shoes from each body. Then, with strips of string, they tied the two great toes together, securing them in death.

Her voice broke the silence. "Why are you doing that?" she asked softly, curiosity flickering even through her grief.

An older man, his face weathered like the land itself, glanced at her and gave a faint, solemn smile.

"It is so their bodies and their souls cannot be invaded again. It is our way, child. Our way of giving them peace after dying in vain."

Marco tilted his head, his small voice barely above a whisper. "What does 'vain' mean?"

The man chuckled sadly, ruffling Marco's hair with a tenderness that masked his pain. "You'll understand when you're older, little one. For now, just remember, we honor them this way so their suffering ends here."

The children said nothing more. They simply watched, wide-eyed and silent, as their parents and neighbors were prepared for their final rest. In that moment, surrounded by rituals older than memory, Thalía and Marco understood one thing clearly:

They were alive. And because they were alive, they carried the weight of all who no longer were.

CHAPTER 5

Coping

The days that followed were heavy with silence. The smoke of grief still lingered over the village, its ashes woven into every home, every whispered prayer, every cautious breath. Marco and Thalía, two children whose innocence had been stolen in a single night, now found themselves under the care of survivors who carried their own wounds yet refused to abandon them.

The adults tried their best, offering comfort where words often failed. They taught the children small routines—fetching water, sharing meals, tending to animals in hopes that familiarity would mend what tragedy had shattered. But healing came slowly, if at all. Marco rarely spoke, his wide eyes darting as if expecting another burst of gunfire. Thalía, though trembling inside, wore a mask of strength, clutching her cousin's hand with a fierce determination that seemed far too mature for her young age.

Life was harder now. Resources were scarce, and every act of kindness stretched the villagers thinner. Among them was Camilla, a strong-willed woman who, despite her hesitations, welcomed the children into her already burdened home. She had her own three little ones to feed and protect, yet something in her heart would not allow her to leave Marco and Thalía to fate.

Still, survival in a poverty-stricken community torn apart by mercenaries and drug lords was no easy task. Food was limited.

Clothes were patched and re-patched until the fabric nearly dissolved. Love, though abundant in spirit, often had to be rationed in practice. And though Marco and Thalía were grateful, they could not escape the gnawing ache of being third and fourth in line, receiving what remained after Camilla's children were tended to.

Through it all, Thalía's resolve hardened. She missed her parents desperately, but she knew the truth; she knew they would never come back. And so she built her shield, a façade of strength to mask the sorrow that clawed at her heart. For Marco's sake, she had no choice. She had always loved her cousin, always chased him through the fields, always played beside him in the barns, always laughed as they brushed the horses and scattered feed to the wild animals on the edge of the village. But now her love had taken on a new weight: she was his protector, his anchor, his guide through the storm.

Marco, though small and soft-spoken, carried his own spark of resilience. Quick on his feet, eager to kick a soccer ball with anyone willing to play, he sought moments of joy where he could find them. And when the other children turned away, mocking their strange eyes (their heterochromia), Thalía stood by his side, demanding he be chosen, refusing to let him be cast aside.

Hunger remained a cruel teacher. More often than not, scraps from the table became their portion. On nights when Marco's stomach still ached, Thalía would quietly slide part of her share onto his plate. He hated taking from her, hated seeing her go hungry, but she would only smile faintly and whisper, *"Eat, Marco. You need it more than I do."*

It was in these small, quiet sacrifices, in the unspoken bond between them that the children began to cope. They could not erase the horrors they had seen, nor bring back the family they had lost. But together, they clung to survival. Together, they forged strength from sorrow. And together, even in the darkest nights, they carried the faint spark of hope that tomorrow might be kinder.

CHAPTER 6

Moving Forward

The years did not pass quickly, but they passed nonetheless. Thalía and Marco, once fragile children, trembling in the shadows of loss, were now two souls learning how to survive in a world that had shown them both cruelty and resilience.

Their new home was far from ideal. A cramped closet under the stairs, no larger than a storage space, became their sanctuary. In the darkness of that little room, they whispered their fears, shared their dreams, and held onto one another as the rest of the world seemed determined to move forward without them. By this time, nearly two years had slipped by. Thalía now approaching ten years old and Marco eight. The two cousins, bound not only by blood but by tragedy, leaned on each other for strength in ways no child ever should have to.

Despite the hardships, they carried gratitude in their hearts. They knew Camilla and Jared, though stretched thin with their own burdens, had taken them in when no one else could. The food was sometimes meager, the affection divided, but it was still more than the cold emptiness of being alone.

At least once every couple of weeks, the cousins made the solemn walk to the gravesite where their parents rested beneath the earth. Together they knelt, praying, grieving, and recalling the warmth of happier days—the laughter of their families, the afternoons spent chasing animals through the fields, the comfort of a mother's embrace. Those visits kept the memories alive and gave them the strength to push forward, even when their stomachs were empty or their hearts heavy.

Meanwhile, the village itself began to breathe again. The scars of the raid still marked its people, but hope flickered in the ruins. Determined to restore some sense of normalcy, Camilla and Jared decide to repair the old saloon that had been badly damaged in the raid, and the owner killed by the mercenaries. It was more than just a place for food and drink, it was a symbol of resilience, a gathering space where laughter could once again echo, where music could drown out the ghosts of gunfire, and where the villagers could remember that joy was still possible.

Six more months passed, and the saloon became a centerpiece of village life. Its walls, once weathered and broken, now hummed with voices, music, and the clinking of glasses. To keep it running, everyone had to pitch in including Thalía and Marco. The two were enlisted to sweep floors, wash dishes, and handle odd jobs around the place. It was hard work, but it kept them busy, distracted from their grief, and slowly integrated them into the pulse of a community attempting to move forward.

By now, the two kids had begun to blossom and getting used to the new norm.

Fate would not abandon them. One morning out of nowhere, the children awoke to find a group of humanitarian workers from the United States who had come to bring aid to their village. Among their many acts of compassion, they offered the children a humble yet life-changing gift—contact lenses. With a *single lens*, both eyes became the same warm shade of brown, and the mockery and stares that once shadowed them began to disappear. The taunts and ridicule from the other children began to fade.

The cousins felt a measure of peace. Their hearts overflowed with gratitude toward the Americans whose kindness had reached their forgotten corner of the world. The visitors brought food, medicine, and other essentials for survival. For Thalía and the villagers, it was more than generosity, it was a glimpse of hope, a flicker of light that awakened a dream.

The rhythm of daily life began to feel almost normal. And though the shadows of the past still lingered, Thalía and Marco held tightly to each other, knowing that moving forward did not mean forgetting, it meant finding the courage to build something new on the ashes of what had been lost.

CHAPTER 7

Unwelcomed Characters

The saloon had brought life back to the village. Laughter echoed from the barn-turned-gathering-place, music drifted through the warm air, and villagers came to escape the weight of past horrors. Yet with this new energy came shadows—unwelcome visitors drawn from neighboring villages, travelers passing through, and those seeking distractions in drink, violence, or worse. Arguments broke out over spilled drinks, fights erupted over pride or insults, and whispers of prostitution and drug use began threading through the corners of the saloon. The villagers remembered the nightmare of years past and feared it might repeat.

One sunny afternoon, Thalía and Marco were walking their familiar path to their parents' gravesite for their usual visit. The air smelled of earth and wildflowers, a small comfort amidst lingering sorrow. On the way back, they noticed a peculiar figure headed in the direction of the village: a man dressed entirely in black, with a scary-looking scar on his face, a wide-brimmed cowboy hat marked by a unique emblem, mounted on a dark horse pulling a medium-sized wagon.

The man's gaze fell on the children. He tipped his hat slightly, a slow, deliberate smile spreading across his face. "Howdy," he called, his voice casual yet edged with something unsettling. "Hi, kiddo's. *I'm João. What's your name?"*

Thalía and Marco instinctively held each other tighter, quickening their pace without a word. The man merely smirked, a glint of amusement in his eyes, and continued on toward the town.

Later, when the cousins arrived back at the saloon for work, they saw João at the bar—drinking. The moment their eyes met, a chill ran down Thalía's spine. That ugly scar on his face could not have come from something good, it had "bad intentions" written all over it. His gaze lingered, unsettling in a way she could not shake.

Throughout the day, João roved the saloon, camera in hand, advertising that he is a photographer for a magazine. He explained that his company sent him to small towns to look for everyday people to photograph. If their picture turned out good enough, he said, they might be featured in the magazine and earn a little extra money. Thalía noticed he only spoke to certain people, mostly women, and she felt a flicker of unease that he hadn't yet approached her, or perhaps had chosen to ignore her deliberately.

Finally, one of the working girls approached her. "He wants to take your photo," she whispered. Reluctant but curious, Thalía said ok. João approached Thalía, raised his camera, studying her with the same unnerving intensity. "Beautiful. Just beautiful," he murmured, lowering the camera briefly. "You'll do just fine."

Thalía's stomach all of a sudden felt twisted. She didn't understand what he meant, but the tone of his words made her instinctively pull back. When he asked her to pose in ways that made her uncomfortable, she shook her head firmly. "No. That's enough," she said, stepping away. Those nearby overheard and exchanged uneasy glances.

As the day continued, João's presence became more menacing. Thalía confided in Jared, telling him she felt unsafe, but he waved it off. "Ignore him. Keep working," Jared said.

When Thalía reached for a glass near João at the bar, he suddenly grabbed her hand. "What's your name, little girl?" he said, a devilish grin spreading across his face. She yanked her hand free and ran for Camilla, then warned Marco to stay clear of him. João laughed, a chilling sound that followed them into the back of the saloon.

Jared called Marco to the back of the kitchen to bring him some clean silverware. Both Thalía and Marco were reluctant for him to go, but because Jared needed it he knew he didn't have a choice. Camilla told Marco that it's OK, he's safe here in the saloon. As Marco walked through the small remote hallway to deliver the silverware, João, drunk and dangerous, ambushed him. He puts his hand over his mouth so he couldn't scream and forced him into the restroom. João pulled out his knife and said, "if you scream, I will cut your throat!" Marco was so terrified, but he fought, resisted, and wouldn't comply with what João wanted him to do.

Thalía, sensing something was wrong, followed the timing closely. When Marco did not return, she went to check and heard a scuffle from the men's restroom. Bursting in, she saw João grabbing and pulling her cousin—Marco scuffling, fighting, and resisting. She screamed for help, Camilla and Jared arrived immediately. João, realizing the danger, fled through a window, leaving Marco shaken but unharmed.

In the days that followed, the man in the black hat (João) was nowhere to be seen. Relief washed over the Thalía and Marco, though the threat of his return lingered in their minds like a shadow.

Soon after, the village buzzed with grim conversations—children and young adults missing, posters hung across streets, a stark reminder that danger still prowled quietly in the corners of their world.

Attempts to involve local authorities yielded no help.

Because the majority of the missing were from poor families, or prostitutes, no one with authority really showed too much concern or paid any attention.

"If you can't pay up," one officer said facetiously, "there's nothing I can, or will do!" He walked away, leaving fear and frustration in his wake.

Thalía and Marco, once again, were reminded that survival in their world required vigilance, courage, and the unwavering support of each other. The darkness had returned in a new form, and they would have to face it, together. They couldn't help but think, that if they weren't so poor and had money to pay, the authorities would have bent over backwards to find out about these missing people.

CHAPTER 8

Rising Shadows

The village seemed quieter after João disappeared, but the calm was deceptive. Shadows lingered in the corners of alleys, whispers of missing children still haunted conversations, and every unfamiliar face passing through the saloon was scrutinized by wary eyes. Thalía and Marco had learned the hard truth: danger could strike at any moment, and relying on adults alone was no longer enough.

Thalía, carried the weight of responsibility with quiet determination. She watched the villagers carefully, noting who came and went, who lingered too long, and whose behavior seemed off. Marco, though younger, matched her vigilance with speed and cunning. His athleticism and sharp instincts allowed him to notice details others overlooked. Together, they became an unseen pair of sentinels, their bond forged in tragedy and strengthened through survival.

Camilla and Jared, while providing a safe home, were busy with the saloon and village responsibilities. The children knew they could not rely on them to act immediately. So, they devised their own system: signals, lookout points, and safe spots within the barn and surrounding streets. They memorized escape routes, hiding spots, and the paths João had taken when he fled. Every step was calculated, every glance intentional.

One evening, as the sun dipped behind distant hills, Thalía and Marco sat on the roof of the barn, overlooking the village. The wind carried the smell of smoke and earth, and the laughter of villagers echoed faintly from the saloon below.

"Do you think he'll come back?" Marco asked, his voice tight with concern.

Thalía's gaze didn't waver. "Maybe. But we won't be caught off guard again." She rested her hand on his shoulder. "We survived him once. We'll survive him again. And this time, we won't just hide. We'll be ready."

The two cousins spent weeks quietly observing, noting who might pose a threat, and helping Camilla and Jared enforce safer practices in the saloon. They moved with stealth, blending into shadows while keeping an eye on the newcomers. Thalía's eyes scanned every face, reading intentions before words were spoken. Marco, smaller but lightning-fast, practiced diversion tactics and emergency signals, often turning play into preparation.

But it wasn't all fear and vigilance. In stolen moments, they played fútbol in the fields, chased the village animals, and laughed quietly together, holding onto the fragments of childhood that still belonged to them. These moments became their armor, giving them the courage to face the growing darkness with a strength that belied their years.

One day, from the edge of the village, a group of travelers arrived. Thalía spotted one man in particular—a tall figure, unfamiliar, eyes darting suspiciously toward the saloon. Her stomach tightened. The same instinct that had warned her about João flared to life.

"This isn't a coincidence," she whispered to Marco, "He's scouting. We need to be ready."

Marco nodded silently, understanding the weight behind her words. The game had changed. The village's safety, their own survival, now depended on their courage, their intelligence, and the unbreakable bond between them.

As night fell, the cousins slipped into their lookout positions, hearts pounding, eyes scanning every shadow. The world had taught them that peace was fleeting, but so long as they stood together, they were prepared to face whatever shadows crept toward their lives next.

CHAPTER 9

The Threat Returns

The evening air hung heavy, carrying with it the smell of roasted maize and woodsmoke from the saloon. Music and laughter spilled into the night, but beneath it all, Thalía felt something wrong, a discordant note only she and Marco seemed to hear.

The tall stranger she had noticed days before sat in the corner of the saloon, his back against the wall, his eyes sharp as a blade. He drank little, spoke even less, but watched everything. His boots were dusty, his jacket too fine for a passing traveler, and when he thought no one noticed, his hand brushed the outline of a pistol beneath his coat.

Thalía whispered to Marco as they cleared the tables nearby, "He doesn't belong here. Look at the way he's watching Jared count the money."

Marco's eyes darted over, sharp and quick. "And he hasn't taken a sip of that drink in an hour. He's not here for the music."

The cousins exchanged a glance. Instinct told them what the villagers could not yet see: danger had returned, cloaked in patience.

That night, while Camilla and Jared closed the saloon, Thalía and Marco slipped to their lookout point on the barn roof they they had created. The stranger had left quietly, but they followed from the shadows, bare feet silent on dirt roads. They kept their distance, hearts racing, until they saw him stop near the tree line at the edge of the village. There, in the moonlight, he met with two other men, faces unfamiliar, but the weapons slung over their shoulders spoke volumes.

Thalía's breath caught. "He's not alone."

Marco swallowed hard. "Three of them. Maybe more." His voice shook, but his eyes were steady. "They're planning something."

The men's muffled voices carried in the night air. Though the words were indistinct, the intent was unmistakable: a return of violence, a raid waiting to happen.

Suddenly, one of the men glanced toward the village and caught the faintest flicker of movement in the shadows. Marco yanked Thalía down just in time, hearts pounding as the men scanned the area. For a long, tense moment, the cousins lay in the dirt, motionless. Finally, the strangers turned back toward the hills, disappearing into the dark.

Only when silence returned did Marco exhale. "They almost saw us."

Thalía clenched her fists. "But now we know. We can warn the village." Her voice hardened with a resolve far beyond her years. "This time, we won't wait for them to strike. We'll be ready."

The cousins hurried back, whispering their plan as adrenaline surged through their veins. They would tell Camilla and Jared, yes, but they also knew the villagers could not depend solely on the adults to defend them. Thalía and Marco had spent weeks preparing, quietly building a system of signals and escape routes. Now, it was time to put those lessons into action.

The shadows were no longer creeping at the edges. They were marching closer, bringing danger back to their doorstep.

But Thalía and Marco were no longer helpless children. They were watchful, bonded by fire and grief, and ready to stand against the darkness.

Poor Little Poor Girl

CHAPTER 10

Preparing for the Storm

The next morning, the saloon was quieter than usual. Jared noticed it first, the children weren't joking or smiling as they worked, and their eyes kept darting toward the door. Camilla caught on quickly, sensing the weight of something unspoken.

Finally, Thalía stepped forward, her voice steady but urgent.

"Last night we followed the stranger. He isn't here to drink or dance. He met with two others, armed men. They're planning something… something against the village."

The words dropped like stones into the room. Jared's face darkened, and Camilla set down the pot she was washing with trembling hands.

"Are you certain?" Jared asked.

Marco nodded. "We saw them with rifles. They know the village is thriving again, that people gather here at the saloon. That makes us a target."

For a long moment, silence gripped the room. Then Jared stood, his voice carrying the weight of leadership.

"Then we prepare. We will not let the darkness swallow us again."

* * *

Resilience is Virtue...

Word spread quickly. By afternoon, the villagers had gathered in the barn, the same place where their fears had once taken shelter during previous reign's of terror. Now, it became a war council.

The elders muttered prayers under their breath. Mothers clutched their children's hands tightly. Men sharpened machetes and checked the few rifles that remained from the old days. The air was thick with unease, but also something new, resolve.

Thalía and Marco shared what they had seen, then revealed the network of escape routes and warning signals they had secretly devised over the months. The villagers listened, astonished. What had once been seen as "children's games" now revealed itself as strategy born of survival.

"If they come through the east road," Marco explained, "we light a lantern in the bell tower. If they come from the hills, we bang the iron against the water tank. Everyone will know what to do."

"And the children?" Camilla asked, her voice breaking.

Thalía's eyes softened, but her tone was firm. "They go to the old caves by the river. We'll lead them ourselves if we have to."

The plan settled over the villagers like a shield. They refused to wait and be victims again, they were preparing to fight back.

That night, as the lanterns burned low in the saloon, Thalía and Marco stood side by side at the doorway, watching the horizon. The jungle was alive with sound, but their hearts listened for something else: footsteps, gunfire, the crack of branches that did not belong.

Marco broke the silence. "Do you think we're ready?"

Thalía's mouth tightened, her eyes fixed on the darkness. "We have to be. This village has already lost too much. We won't let it happen again."

And as the first distant howl of a dog split the night, both cousins felt it, the storm was coming.

Poor Little Poor Girl

CHAPTER 11

The Raid

It began just before dawn.

A sharp whistle cut through the silence, followed by the thunder of boots on dirt. The raiders descended from the hills, their rifles gleaming in the pale light. The first shots shattered the stillness of the village, sending birds screeching into the sky.

"East road!" Marco shouted, racing to the bell tower. His hands trembled, but he struck the lantern high and lit the flame. Within seconds, the iron clang of the water tank echoed through the village, every warning signal alive at once.

Chaos erupted. Mothers herded children toward the caves. Men and women, armed with machetes, pitchforks, and the few shotguns left from old battles, poured into the streets.

The raiders fired wildly, their bullets tearing through wooden walls and shattering windows. The saloon, once a place of music and laughter, shook as gunfire punched through its walls. Camilla dragged two frightened children behind the bar, shielding them with her body.

But this time, the villagers were not helpless.

From the rooftops, Jared and two others fired back, picking off the raiders as they tried to charge into the square. Marco ran between houses, shouting instructions, guiding people into their defensive positions just as he and Thalía had planned.

Thalía herself stood in the center of the square, gripping a torch wrapped in oil-soaked cloth. As a group of raiders stormed forward, she hurled it into a cart of dry hay. Flames exploded upward, blocking their path.

"They won't take us alive!" she screamed, her voice carrying through the smoke.

The villagers roared in response, courage rising with the fire.

* * *

The battle raged for what felt like hours, though it was only minutes. Bullets cracked, blades clashed, smoke and screams filled the air. But the raiders had not expected resistance, not from a village they thought broken and weak.

One by one, they fell. Some fled into the trees, others dropped their weapons when cornered by furious farmers wielding nothing but machetes and resolve.

Finally, as the sun rose fully over the horizon, the last shot rang out. Silence followed. The raiders were gone, defeated, scattered, humiliated.

* * *

The villagers gathered in the square, their faces streaked with sweat, dirt, and tears. The saloon stood battered but unbroken. Camilla emerged from the doorway with the children safe at her side. Jared lowered his rifle and breathed out like he'd been holding that breath forever.

Thalía stood beside Marco, her chest heaving, her face smudged with ash but her eyes fierce. She looked at the horizon where the raiders had vanished.

"We did it," Marco whispered, almost in disbelief.

"We did," Thalía said softly, gripping his hand. "We survived, we fought back!"

The villagers raised their voices in cheers, a sound louder than the gunfire had been. After all the pain, hope finally felt louder than fear.

The raid had failed.

The village had triumphed.

And the children who once stood frozen in blood now stood as leaders in fire.

CHAPTER 12

Unfortunate Illnesses

Time had moved forward, but the saloon, once a symbol of renewal, was no longer the pride of the village. Its walls echoed with laughter that had grown hollow, drowned by the clinking of bottles, the slurred voices of drunken men, and the whispers of darker dealings.

By now, Thalía had begun to blossom into a striking young woman. Her features, once shadowed by sorrow, were softening with strength and resilience. Though only thirteen, she carried herself with quiet dignity, and maturity. Her heterochromatic eyes reflecting both the pain she had endured and the fire that still burned within her.

Marco, though younger, was no less determined. His small frame held boundless energy, and his loyalty to Thalía never wavered. Where she went, he followed; where she faltered, he lifted her up. Together, they were not just surviving—they were learning to live again.

Thalía and Marco still worked there faithfully, but the burden was heavy. They were still children, yet in the unstable environment, Thalía was constantly forced to endure the stares, gestures, and unwelcome advances of older men. Their protests to Jared and Camilla were frequent and desperate, but they fell on deaf ears.

"Stay focused," Jared would say. "The saloon is feeding all of us."

Camilla, though weary, only nodded. The money was too good, the business too busy. Neither of them wanted to face the truth—that the very walls of the saloon were becoming a breeding ground for corruption and danger.

* * *

With the influx of strangers from distant villages, something more sinister than drunkenness and violence crept into the community: sickness. Disease moved quietly among the travelers, passed hand to hand, mouth to mouth, bed to bed. Without proper doctors or medicines, infection spread like fire through dry fields.

Marco was the first to fall. One morning, he could no longer rise from bed. His body burned with fever, his skin clammy and pale. The boy who once sprinted barefoot across the fields, who laughed louder than anyone when playing fútbol, now lay weak and trembling, unable to even lift his head.

Thalía begged for medicine, for help, but there was none to give. She pressed cool rags against his forehead, whispered stories to keep his spirit strong, and prayed silently that he would not be taken from her as her parents had been.

Two weeks later, fate struck again. Camilla fell sick with the same symptoms. She, too, became bed-stricken, her coughs echoing through the house like a grim reminder that sickness respected no one.

* * *

The burden fell on Jared and Thalía.

Jared threw himself into running the saloon, but the pressure mounted quickly. Without Camilla's steady hand or Marco's small but eager help, the work consumed him. Business began to slip away.

And so, in desperation, Jared allowed darker things to seep further into his establishment. Prostitution was no longer just tolerated, it was accepted. Drug dealers were given space in shadowed corners. Every vice was welcomed, as long as it brought money to keep the saloon alive.

The cost of that decision, however, was borne by Thalía.

She worked twice as hard, running from table to table, washing, cleaning, keeping order where she could—all while worrying about Marco and Camilla lying sick at home. The exhaustion in her young body grew heavy, but the heavier weight was Jared's cruelty.

He blamed Marco for Camilla's sickness.

"You brought this into my house!" Jared spat one night, his face twisted with anger. "If it weren't for you, she'd still be well!"

Thalía stood between them, her eyes blazing. "It's not his fault! He's just a child!"

But Jared refused to listen. He turned cold, neglectful, shutting his heart to both cousins. To him, they were no longer blessings he had reluctantly taken in—they were curses, reminders of suffering, burdens he had not chosen.

* * *

Thalía, however, refused to break. Though the saloon was crumbling around her, Jared grew harder and colder. As her cousin was wasting away in fever, she carried the weight on her narrow shoulders.

For Marco, for Camilla, for the memory of her parents, she endured.

But deep down, she knew: if sickness did not claim them, the darkness growing inside the saloon surely would.

Then, slowly, Camilla's condition began to change. Though still weak, her fever broke one morning, and a hint of color returned to her face. Eleanor, a kind-hearted woman who had been checking in during the illness, took notice and sat with Jared one evening outside the saloon.

She says, "Here's a tip from my grandma—and who knows how many grandmas before her. Most people don't even realize this, but she always said to change your toothbrush every three days. All those nasty germs and bacteria collect on it and just keep the virus going."

Jared pauses for a few second and says, "Hmm, now that makes sense, you're right, I never thought about that". "I'll be sure to tell Thalía to let them know".

She says, "So now that I have your attention, here's something else I'm right about".

"You're carrying too much, Jared," she told him softly. "But anger won't heal anyone. Thalía and Marco aren't the cause of this suffering, they're victims of it too. You've let your grief and your fear blind you."

Jared sat in silence, his calloused hands trembling. He thought of Thalía's weary face, of Marco's frail body lying in the bed, and of how quickly he had cast his blame upon them. The truth struck him harder than any blow: he had failed them.

That night, Jared approached the children. Thalía instinctively braced herself, expecting another scolding, but instead his voice broke with guilt.

"I... I was wrong," Jared admitted, lowering his eyes. "The stress of it all—the saloon, the sickness, losing control, I let it twist me. I should never have taken it out on you two." His voice faltered, but he forced the words through. "I'm sorry, Thalía. I'm sorry, Marco."

Thalía's stern face softened, though tears welled in her eyes. Marco, still weak, only managed a faint nod, but the forgiveness in his gaze was enough.

For the first time in many weeks, the heaviness in the house lifted, if only slightly. Camilla smiled faintly from her bed, whispering that the family must stay together no matter the trials.

And in that fragile moment, hope returned, thin as glass, but shining all the same.

Poor Little Poor Girl

CHAPTER 13

Introducing... Eleanor

Eleanor was a woman forged by fire (*a Baddass*). A survivor of a world where cruelty reigned and mercy was a forgotten luxury. Before the drug lords stormed through these lands, she had been the Madam of a brothel in a neighboring village, running her business with sharp wit and an iron will. But when the missionaries came, the same who promised salvation at the barrel of a gun, they left only destruction in their wake. They burned the house of work to ashes, slaughtered many of her girls, and kidnapped others into slavery. Eleanor survived, but survival came at a cost.

With only a handful of her remaining girls left, she crossed into Jared's village, swallowing her pride to make a new bargain. She offered Jared a cut of the profits if he let her set up business within his saloon. He, desperate for income, agreed. Thus, Eleanor found herself rebuilding in the ashes of her past, doing what she had always done—enduring, fighting, and keeping her people alive.

Though hardened by circumstance, Eleanor was not heartless. She was vigilant, fiercely protective of the women she employed. She had seen too many wolves in men's clothing, too many "customers" who thought desperation meant weakness. But Eleanor had learned long ago that weakness was a mask she never wore.

Thalía and Marco learned this one unforgettable evening.

A drunk man, towering over Eleanor, had laid hands on one of her girls, cursing and shoving her aside. Eleanor's eyes sharpened, her voice cutting through the chaos like steel. "LEAVE HER ALONE" she shouted. As she approached the guy, he says to her. "Mind your damn business lady!"

"This is my business," she warned.

The man sneered. "Shut up, bitch," he spat, and swung at her.

But Eleanor was faster. She ducked beneath his swing, snatched a bottle from the counter, and smashed it across his skull. The saloon erupted in gasps as the brute stumbled back, dazed. Jared and a few others seized the moment, dragging the drunk into the street.

Thalía and Marco stared wide-eyed, their young minds stunned by the sheer fire in Eleanor's defiance. That night, they realized she was no ordinary woman.

And she proved it again not long after.

When two knife-wielding men stormed the saloon during a slow shift, demanding money from Carlos, the apathetic hired hand— Eleanor didn't hesitate. With her girls' livelihoods on the line, she stepped forward.

In her heels and dress, she ripped off her shoes, swung a chair across one robber's head, and sent him sprawling. The second man tackled her, but Eleanor twisted, reversed the hold, and rained fists upon him until his grip faltered. The first attacker staggered back to his feet, blood dripping from his face, only to receive a sharp kick to the gut and a crushing punch to the nose. He fell howling, blinded by blood and tears. Eleanor finished him with a brutal crack of another bottle.

The second man tried once more, but Eleanor's backhand smashed across his face, dropping him to the ground. By then her girls swarmed in, kicking the robbers into the street like broken dogs.

And through it all, Carlos (the man) merely stood by, watching with indifference. Not a move to help. Not a word to protect. Eleanor's instincts immediately flared. Later on she told Jared, "That one isn't right. Keep your eye on him. He smells like betrayal." Jared only nodded, but the warning lingered.

The next day, Thalía and Marco caught Eleanor outside the saloon, their faces bright with awe.

"How did you fight like that?" they blurted in unison.

Eleanor chuckled, a rare softness cracking her hardened shell. "I used to date an American. A martial arts instructor. Taught me a few tricks. Around here, a woman doesn't stay alive long if she can't defend herself." She winked. "And trust me, I've had to use those moves more times than I can count."

Thalía's eyes lit up. "Will you teach me? Please?!"

Marco jumped in, eager. "Me too, me too! I want to learn!"

For a moment, Eleanor hesitated. But looking at the two cousins, orphans bound together by loss and resilience, her heart softened. She placed a hand on each of their shoulders. "Of course. You deserve to know how to protect yourselves. If I teach you, maybe I won't have to worry so much."

From then on, Eleanor became more than the saloon's guardian. She became *Tía Eleanor to them*. She trained Thalía and Marco in secret moments, turning playful games into instinctive lessons. A jab disguised as a joke. A kick softened to a nudge. Overtime, their reflexes sharpened, and laughter often followed their mock sparring matches.

She watched them from a distance too, always alert, always protective. For Eleanor knew the dangers lurking in the saloon's shadows. She knew what men were capable of when drink and darkness mingled. And though she had built her life on survival, she now found herself living for something else, for two children who reminded her that even in a world drenched in sin and blood, there was still innocence worth defending.

In their laughter, Eleanor saw hope. And hope was something she hadn't felt in years.

As Eleanor watched Thalía and Marco race down the dirt road that evening, still laughing from their "training," she smiled, a rare, genuine smile that reached her weary eyes. But when she turned back toward the saloon, her expression hardened.

Carlos leaned against the doorframe, his arms crossed, watching her with an unreadable look. He had barely lifted a finger during the attempted robbery, yet now his eyes lingered on her and the children in a way that made her skin crawl.

Eleanor narrowed her gaze. Her instincts had kept her alive this long, and they were whispering again now. Something about Carlos wasn't right. Something told her the storm wasn't over. As if he may have even been in cahoots with the robbers.

She muttered under her breath, almost like a promise:

"If he ever threatens those kids, he'll regret the day he was born."

And in that quiet vow, a shift occurred. Eleanor wasn't just a survivor anymore, she had become a guardian.

CHAPTER 14

The Unthinkable

One late afternoon, after milking the cow and tending to Marco and Camilla, Thalía reported to the saloon to help Jared. She immediately noticed how overwhelmed he looked, sweat on his brow, frustration etched across his face, as customers crowded every table and lined the bar.

Then, across the room, her heart froze.

Seated at the bar was a familiar figure who resembled João, the man in black. Only now, he wasn't cloaked head-to-toe in darkness; he wore lighter clothes, but still had on the black hat with its sinister emblem—twisted into the shape of a snake coiled around a goat's skull. He presented a foolish attempt to cover his scar with a bandanna, but his presence was unmistakable, his aura poisonous.

He pulled out a wad of money and waved it lazily, his eyes locking on her. With a devilish grin, he called out, "Come here, niña. I need a drink."

Thalía froze, glancing toward Jared. He gave a small nod, silently urging her to serve the man. Reluctantly, she moved toward him.

Before she could reach him, Eleanor realized it actually was indeed João, but had grown his beard in an attempt to cover the scar and disguise his appearance. Eleanor intercepted, her stance firm. "She's not for sale," she said, her voice sharp as steel.

João looked between Eleanor and Thalía, that grin never faltering. "Everyone has a price," he chuckled, his signature laugh crawling through the air like a vulture's cry.

The night dragged on with chaos—drunken shouts, clinking glasses, the usual storm of the saloon. At last, Jared released Thalía to return home and care for the sick. Relieved, she hurried back, tending to Camilla and Marco as best she could.

But later, both Camilla and Marco needed fresh water. With no choice, Thalía steeled herself and returned to the saloon for more.

She prayed João would be gone.

Her prayer went unanswered.

There he was, leaning at the entrance, smoking a cigar, the ember glowing like a watchful eye. His grin widened as she passed. Thalía forced herself inside quickly, fetched the water, and reassured Jared that Camilla and Marco were showing small signs of improvement. Jared patted her head softly. "Good girl. Thank you. That's a relief."

With the water in hand, Thalía slipped out, heart pounding. The entrance was clear. João was no longer standing there. She exhaled in relief and set off toward home, walking fast enough to spill droplets from the jug. She slowed down, not wanting to lose what little water she carried.

Then—movement.

From between two buildings, a shadow emerged. João. His eyes glinted as he stepped into her path.

Fear clutched her chest. She tried to quicken her pace, but he matched her stride. Then he began to chase.

Her feet pounded the earth as she sprinted, the water sloshing and spilling. The open field ahead seemed endless, but it was her only path to home. She ran, desperate, until he caught her.

"Well, hello pretty girl," he hissed, yanking her down. His hand cracked across her face. The sting burned as he dragged her into the tall grass. She screamed, kicked, fought, but she was too far out in the field for anyone to hear, and he was too strong.

The world blurred into terror. His grip crushed her arms, his laughter filled her ears. When resistance failed, her body went still, hollow. The fight drained from her, replaced by survival. She lay in the grass, broken, as João committed the unthinkable.

When he was finished, he sneered, kicked her in the ribs, and crouched over her trembling frame.

"If you tell anyone," he growled, "I'll come back for you. I'll kill your cousin, and burn your saloon to the ground!" His laugh cut through the night; low, cruel, unforgettable. "Be grateful I'm already... satisfied."

And then he was gone, swallowed into the dark.

Shaking, aching, bruised, Thalía forced herself up. She now had no water for Camilla and Marco, as it all spilled out when she dropped the pail after João smacked her down. She wiped the dirt from her clothes, smeared away her tears, and stumbled back to the saloon through the rear entrance. She filled the jug again, praying no one would see her in this broken state.

Little did she know, Eleanor with her keen instincts, saw her sneaking in and out.

At home, she placed the water down gently. Camilla stirred and Marco blinked weakly at her. Both froze when they saw her bruised face.

"What happened?" Marco whispered, eyes wide. "Why are you hurt?"

Thalía forced a shaky smile. "I slipped. Fell down the hill, while carrying the water." She brushed at the dirt off her clothes. "That's all. Don't worry about me. You two are the ones who need to get better."

Her smile trembled, but she held it because she had no other choice.

CHAPTER 15

Faced with Depression

In the days that followed the night of the unthinkable, Thalía moved through life as if wrapped in a shroud. Her once-bright spirit dimmed into silence. She became quiet, withdrawn, her laughter gone, her smile a mask stretched too thin. When spoken to, she answered with nods or short murmurs, drifting through her chores as if on autopilot.

Jared noticed, but only in the way a man preoccupied with his own burdens might. When the bruises on her face and arms drew his attention, he asked, half-concerned, half-irritated, "What happened this time?"

Each time, Thalía gave the same excuse she had told Camilla and Marco, that she slipped, and fell down the hill. Jared would sigh and shake his head. "You have to be careful," he muttered, the weight of the saloon heavy on his shoulders. "I can't afford to care for another sickling." Then he would move on, blind to the storm unraveling inside her.

But Eleanor was not so easily fooled.

From her perch as head of the working girls, she had seen too much, survived too much, to ignore the signs. Girls had gone missing before, too many. And Eleanor had taken note of João's predatory stare, his sinister laugh, the way he slithered around the saloon. That night, she'd seen him disappear from the porch just after Thalía left with her water jug. Later, when Thalía crept back to the saloon in dirt-stained clothes, Eleanor's suspicion hardened into certainty. She hadn't been close enough to see the bruises, but she didn't need to. Her instincts screamed what her eyes could not yet prove.

Thalía, meanwhile, forced herself to keep moving. Despite the aches in her body, despite the bruises she tried to hide, she tended to Marco and Camilla faithfully. She assumed the role of caretaker with the quiet dignity of someone twice her age, calling Jared and Camilla "Tío" and "Tía" in public to honor the life they had given her and Marco.

But even strength has its cracks.

When she ventured beyond the saloon, the other children her age would point and whisper. Some laughed, mocking her as "the poor girl," a burden taken in only out of pity. A charity case. She said nothing back, never letting her tears show, though the words cut her deeper than the bruises.

In silence, she endured. She shouldered her responsibilities with grit, her love for Marco and Camilla keeping her upright when her soul wanted to collapse. Yet behind her quiet eyes, shadows lingered, growing darker with each passing day.

And Eleanor, sharp-eyed, battle-worn Eleanor, watched. She watched and waited, knowing sooner or later, Thalía's truth would come to light.

CHAPTER 16

Eleanor's Confrontation

The saloon buzzed with its usual chaos—clinking glasses, slurred songs, laughter that always carried an edge of danger. But Eleanor wasn't listening. Her sharp eyes weren't on the crowd; they were on Thalía.

The girl moved like a ghost, silent and efficient, gathering glasses and wiping tables without ever looking up. Her small frame carried a weight far beyond her years, and Eleanor had lived long enough to know that wasn't just grief. Something darker was gnawing at her.

When the night grew late and the crowd thinned, Eleanor made her move. She caught Thalía by the arm as she slipped past with a tray of empty mugs. "Sit," Eleanor ordered softly, her voice calm but firm. She guided her to a quiet corner table away from Jared's eyes.

Thalía tried to protest. "I still have work!"

Eleanor silenced her with a look. "The work can wait. You can't."

For a long moment, they sat in silence. Eleanor leaned back, studying her. "I've been watching you, niña. The bruises, the silence... the way you flinch when certain men come near. You've been lying to Jared. You've been lying to Camilla. And you've been lying to yourself."

Thalía's chest tightened. Her eyes dropped to the table, fingers twisting the hem of her dress. "I fell," she whispered. "That's all."

Eleanor leaned forward, her voice low, steady. "I've seen girls in your shoes before. Too many. And I've buried some of them. Don't lie to me. Not to me."

Tears welled in Thalía's eyes, but she shook her head fiercely. "I can't... I can't say."

Eleanor softened, reaching out to cup Thalía's trembling hand. "Listen to me, child. Whatever happened, it's not your fault. Do you hear me? Not your fault."

Thalía's lips quivered. She wanted to speak, to release the secret poisoning her heart, but João's threats echoed in her mind—his knife, his laughter, his promise to kill Marco, to burn everything. Fear clamped down on her throat like iron.

"I can't," she choked, pulling her hand away. "If I say anything... he'll hurt Marco. He'll hurt all of us."

Eleanor froze. That was all the confirmation she needed. She didn't push further, not yet. Instead, she straightened and fixed Thalía with a gaze both fierce and maternal.

"Then listen to me," she said. "You are not alone. Do you understand? You have me now. If that person, whoever they are, ever comes near you again, they'll answer to me (*Eleanor*), before anyone else."

Thalía blinked at her through tears. After weeks of fear, a sliver of safety finally reached her broken heart. She nodded, swallowing hard, though the fear remained heavy.

Eleanor leaned back, lighting a cigarette with steady hands, her eyes never leaving Thalía. "The world is full of wolves, niña. But even wolves learn to fear when the right hunter comes along."

In that dimly lit saloon, a quiet pact was born—unspoken but binding. Thalía had not confessed everything, but Eleanor knew enough. And one way or another, she would keep that child safe.

As Eleanor lifted her hand to light her cigarette, the glint of a delicate bracelet caught Thalía's eye. A small, silver wing charm dangled from it, shimmering softly in the afternoon light.

"It's so pretty," Thalía said, smiling as she leaned closer.

Eleanor glanced down at it, a faint smile touching her lips. "Thank you, cariño," she said softly. "It's special to me. A gift from someone I once cared for, a man I loved. My martial arts instructor, back when I was younger."

Thalía nodded, her gaze lingering on the bracelet, captivated not just by its shine, but by the quiet emotion behind her *Tía's* words.

CHAPTER 17

Recovery and Discovery

The sickness that had nearly torn the household apart was finally loosening its grip. Camilla, pale but stronger with each passing day, could now sit up and move about, while Marco, still weak and coughing, remained confined to his bed. Though not fully healed, their return to health breathed cautious hope into the family.

Yet hope was not enough to save the saloon. With profits dwindling and Thalía stretched to her limit, Jared had been forced to take a gamble: relying the man he barely knew... Carlos. The same man Eleanor warned him about.

At first, Carlos carried himself like a gift from heaven. He laughed loud, kept the guests entertained, and encouraged them to drink until their coins were spent. But the longer he stayed, the clearer the cracks became. He poured himself drinks without paying, bragged about money he didn't have, and whispered stories of a wife and child he claimed to be chasing up north.

Eleanor witnessed these actions firsthand, and reported it to Jared.

Jared wanted to believe him, wanted to think Carlos was just another desperate soul trying to put his life back together. But Eleanor had warned him more than once: *"Men who drink as he drinks are dangerous. Mark my words."*

What no one knew was that Carlos carried a darker truth. He had not come from a place of honest labor but from a jail cell, his past marked with drunken violence. His wife had fled, not waiting for him to change. Now, in his desperation, he clung to the idea of finding her again, no matter what the cost.

When Camilla, still frail but determined, returned to the saloon, Jared no longer had need of Carlos. One evening, after closing, Jared called him aside.

"You've done enough here," Jared said firmly. "Camilla is back, and besides, I can't afford to keep you anymore."

Carlos's face twisted. "Just another month," he begged. "I need the money to find my family. Don't take this from me."

But Jared shook his head. "You've already taken too much. You've stolen from the register. You've stolen from Eleanor's girls. And you've stolen from me every time you poured yourself a drink without paying."

The air went cold. Carlos's pleading turned to rage. He stepped forward, his voice rising. "I'm the reason this place even has customers! You think you'll survive without me? When I'm gone, this saloon will rot in the dirt."

Jared stood his ground. "Better that than be bled dry by a thief!"

Fury flared in Carlos's eyes, and for a moment, it seemed fists— or worse—would be drawn. But Jared didn't flinch. The silence stretched before Carlos spat at the floor, his voice seething with threat.

"You'll regret this. I'll make sure of it."

He stormed out into the night, the saloon's lanterns casting his shadow long and crooked against the dirt road.

Later, Eleanor found Jared at the bar, staring into his empty glass. She placed a hand on his shoulder. "You did the right thing. That man had poison in his veins. My girls saw him with drugs, saw him stealing money. Letting him go might've just saved us more trouble than we can imagine."

But her words, meant to reassure, only deepened the unease twisting in Jared's gut. Because he knew men like Carlos, the kind who never left quietly.

Jared says to Eleanor, "Can you believe he had the nerve to threaten me—saying he'd tell Camilla that I *let* your girls flirt with me? All I did was let them do their jobs, earn their tips, and keep business moving for the saloon. Times are hard around here. A little kindness shouldn't be twisted into something it's not."

Eleanor replied, "You don't need to worry about that asshole. Don't second-guess yourself, you did the right thing by cutting him loose."

I had to do what I had to do," Jared says.

"Then he tried to justify it by saying that's just how he's *perceived* things since he started working here. I can't believe he used that one phrase I hate more than anything."

'What phrase?' Eleanor asks.

"He said, *perception is reality!"*

Eleanor goes off! "I hate that stupid phrase too! People twist it all the time. They always use it in the most negative way possible. Look—*perception is in the eye of the beholder.* If someone's has a rotten, devious core, and bad intentions, then of course their perception will be just as wicked."

"But if someone is decent and kind, their perception will reflect that instead. And that's the God-honest truth!"

63

Jared was taken aback by her reaction; it was clear Eleanor had some personal history with that phrase. He didn't interrupt—he simply listened, nodding with quiet confidence as she vented.

And as the village settled into uneasy silence that night, a question hung heavy in the air: had Jared rid himself of a burden, or awakened an enemy that would come back with vengeance?

CHAPTER 18

The Trap

Days passed, and the household began to breathe again. Marco's strength returned enough for him to help with chores, and Camilla, though still pale, joined Jared and Thalía back at the saloon. The four of them worked side by side, fighting to restore the business that sickness had nearly broken.

Carlos lingered around town, lurking like a stray dog no one wanted to feed. Though Jared had dismissed him, he hadn't left. He kept to the edges, quiet, harmless, or so it seemed.

That afternoon, Thalía and Marco were out in the pasture, milking the cow as the sun slid toward the horizon. Suddenly, Marco's head jerked up. "Thalía…" he whispered.

Over the hill, silhouetted by the dying light, was the man in the black hat with the scar on his face. The snake-and-skull emblem gleamed faintly from above the brim. João!

Thalía's heart leapt into her throat. She grabbed Marco's hand, and together they bolted into the house, slamming the door and pressing their backs against it, breathless. Neither spoke, but both knew: It was João, he was back!

By nightfall, Thalía tried to push the fear aside. She had duties at the saloon and could not simply abandon Jared and Camilla. She walked the familiar path, lantern in hand, her eyes darting into the shadows at every sound.

Halfway there, she nearly collided with Carlos.

"Thalía," he said, almost too eagerly, "I need a favor. I have some things—money that I owe Jared. I want you to take it to him. And... tell him I'm sorry. Please."

His tone seemed genuine. Thalía, a bit relieved, because now she was with a familiar face that if she João found her en route, she wouldn't be alone.

After all, Carlos knew her, knew her family. He had no reason to hurt her. Thalía hesitated but finally nodded. "Alright. Where are the things?"

He gestured down a narrow lane toward a small, dimly lit flat. "Just there at my flat. Won't take but a minute."

Trust warred with unease inside her. But she followed.

The moment she drew near the flat and Carlos opened the door, a cold shiver ran through her. Her chest tightened, her legs froze. The peeling paint, the broken shutter, the smell of mildew in the air, her heart sank. It was *that* place.

The same flat where her parents' were murdered. The night that had changed her life forever. This was the flat where blood had stained the floorboards, where her screams had gone unanswered.

Her knees trembled. She couldn't move.

And then, as if summoned by her terror, a shadow detached itself from the darkness. Carlos's hand lifted slightly, a subtle signal.

From behind the flat, João emerged.

Thalía's breath hitched, her stomach turned to stone. His black hat caught the lantern light, his grin the same devilish curl she had seen before.

Carlos stepped back, his face unreadable. In that instant, Thalía understood, this was no apology. Carlos had traded her. For money, for drink, for his own escape.

João's eyes gleamed as he advanced. "Pretty girl," he said softly, the same words he had used before. "I told you I'd be back."

Thalía's heart pounded in her chest. The betrayal, the flat, her parents, João's looming presence—all of it swirled together in one nightmarish truth: she had walked straight into a trap.

And this time, João hadn't come just for her. He had come to take her and Marco away forever.

CHAPTER 19

Journey to the Underground

Thalía fought with everything she had, but against two grown men she was no match. Her fists struck air, her kicks were caught mid-swing, and her screams were stifled as a rough cloth was pressed hard over her mouth. The bitter, chemical smell filled her nose and burned her throat. She thrashed violently, but João's hand came down hard across the side of her head. White sparks burst before her eyes, and the world slipped into a dizzy, muffled silence before fading to black.

When she came to, her body jostled with every violent bump of the carriage wheels against rocks and ruts in the dirt road. Her head throbbed. The stale air stank of sweat and fear. As her vision cleared, she realized with horror that she wasn't alone.

Crammed tightly in the wagon with her were nearly twenty other children—boys and girls of varying ages. Wide, tear-streaked eyes stared back at her, hollow with terror. Their small hands were bound, their mouths sealed with tape. It took her only seconds to realize her own wrists and ankles were bound as well. The scratch of the coarse rope cut into her skin with every shift.

The silence inside the wagon was suffocating, broken only by muffled whimpers, sniffles, and the groan of wheels rolling endlessly over the uneven ground. Every now and then, the stench of urine and feces grew sharper, reminding her that they had been trapped too long with no release. The heat pressed down on them like a suffocating blanket, sweat soaking their clothes and plastering their hair to their skin.

Hours blurred into days. The passage of time was marked only by the brief moments when the wagon lurched to a stop. João would swing the doors open, his shadow stretching across their trembling faces. With a mocking smile, he offered them small, rusted tin cups of water, barely enough to wet their lips.

"If any of you try to scream, try to run," he warned in a low growl, letting his knife gleam in the dim light, "I'll slit you open and leave you for the vultures."

His words chilled Thalía's blood. She looked around at the faces beside her, children too terrified to fight, too broken to even whimper loudly. Still, João would crouch down and, in a twisted tone of reassurance, whisper, "Don't be afraid. You'll have a better life than the one you left behind. You'll be worth something now."

The lies were as heavy as the chains around their bodies.

Two endless days dragged by, each minute stretching like an eternity. The children stopped struggling, conserving their strength, their young eyes dulled with hopelessness. Thalía, however, kept her gaze sharp, silently vowing she would not give up, she would not let this be her fate.

Thalía realized the nightmare was only beginning.

CHAPTER 20

Missing you

The same night of the "trap"...

The saloon had began to buzz again with life. Camilla, though still regaining her strength, stood behind the bar with Jared, pouring drinks and greeting customers. Laughter and music filled the room, as things almost felt normal. Business was crawling back, coin by coin, smile by smile.

Unbeknownst to them, a shadow hung over the night.

Thalía had not returned.

Back at the house, Marco swept the floor, humming softly to himself, feeling stronger than he had in days. With every chore he finished, he thought of his cousin. Soon, he told himself, they'd all be together at the saloon again. Soon, life would return to the way it was meant to be.

But as the hours dragged on, the sun sinking beyond the hills and lanterns flickering to life in the saloon, Thalía's absence grew heavier.

Camilla glanced toward the door again and again. Each time it creaked open, hope rushed to her chest, only to collapse into disappointment when it wasn't Thalía.

Jared felt the same gnawing unease. He tried to hide it behind his stern demeanor, but every empty glance toward the entrance betrayed him. "Where is that girl?" he muttered more than once, polishing glasses that were already spotless.

By the end of the evening, Camilla's arms ached from work, her chest tight from worry. She closed out the last table and pulled her shawl tight around her shoulders. "I'm going home," she told Jared, though her voice trembled. "Maybe Thalía fell asleep."

The walk home was long, her steps quick and restless. The night felt wrong—too still, too heavy, the silence broken only by the distant howl of a dog.

As she neared the door, the light from inside flickered. Marco's small face appeared at the window, lighting up at the sight of her. He rushed to greet her, flinging the door open.

"Where's Thalía?" he asked cheerfully, almost teasing. "Let me guess, she stayed behind to help Tío Jared? Must be busy tonight, huh?" He laughed lightly, but there was hope in his voice, expectation.

Camilla froze.

"I was just about to ask you the same thing," she said slowly. Her eyes were wide, her words trembling. "Where IS Thalía?"

The laughter died in Marco's throat. His smile faltered, his face twisted with fear. The air seemed to thicken between them as silence pressed down.

Then both of them, without a word, looked into each other's eyes, their expressions mirroring the same dreadful realization.

Something was wrong. Terribly wrong.

Thalía would never stay away this long without sending word. She was dependable, responsible. She always came back.

Marco's hands began to shake. Camilla's breath came quick and shallow. Together, they rushed into the night, their feet pounding the dirt road, frantically retracing the path toward the saloon.

They didn't speak, because they both already knew the truth.

Thalía wasn't just late.

Thalía was missing.

Poor Little Poor Girl

CHAPTER 21

The Storm Breaks

Marco and Camilla burst through the saloon doors, breathless, their faces pale with dread. The music stopped mid-note, glasses clinked uneasily back onto tables, and the usual rowdy laughter dulled into an uneasy hush. Every eye turned toward them.

Jared, standing behind the bar, frowned. "What is it?" he asked, his voice sharp, almost impatient, until he saw their faces.

"Thalía," Camilla gasped, clutching her shawl at her chest. "She never came home. She never made it here. She's gone!"

The words cracked through the room like thunder.

Jared dropped the glass in his hand. It shattered across the bar top, forgotten. His face went ashen, his mouth opening but no sound escaping.

From across the room, Eleanor rose from her table, her sharp eyes narrowing. "What do you mean she's gone?" she demanded, her voice cutting through the silence like a whip.

Camilla stammered, "She left the house earlier to come help, but she never, she never, " Her words dissolved into trembling breaths.

Marco pushed forward, his small fists clenched. "Someone took her! I know it! She would never just disappear!"

Murmurs erupted in the crowd, whispers hissing like snakes: *The girl's missing. Someone took her. Not safe. Not safe.*

Jared slammed his fist onto the bar. "Enough!" His voice boomed, silencing the chatter. His eyes darted across the room, searching faces, searching shadows, but finding no answers. Sweat beaded his forehead, and for the first time ever, the villagers saw the strong saloonkeeper shaken.

Eleanor stepped closer, her facial expression hard, her fists on her hips. "I knew it," she muttered, her voice low but fierce. "That bastard Carlos. He's been sniffing around. I warned you. I told you he'd try something."

The room erupted again, shouts of anger, fear, men rising to their feet, some demanding action, others shrinking back in dread.

"Silence!" Jared roared again, though his own voice cracked with the weight of it. His eyes flicked to Eleanor. "If it was him… then he's not far. He's bold. Too bold."

Eleanor leaned across the bar, her eyes burning into Jared's. "Then what are we waiting for? If that devil's got her, every minute that passes is a minute too late."

The tension snapped like a whip. Men slammed back chairs, ready to search. Some grabbed bottles, others knives. A storm of chaos swirled inside the saloon, voices clashing—fear, anger, desperation.

In the middle of it all, Marco stood trembling, his small body quaking but his voice steady: "Please. We can't just talk about it. We have to find her." His words, childlike but powerful, cut through the noise.

The saloon stilled again. All eyes went to Jared.

Jared, the man who always had an answer, this time had none. He dragged a hand down his face, torn between fury and fear, between the weight of his responsibilities and the gut-wrenching reality that Thalía—innocent, loyal, irreplaceable Thalía—was in danger.

Eleanor slammed her hand on the bar. "Then I'll go. With or without you. That girl calls me *Tía*, and I'll be damned if I let her vanish into the night without a fight."

Elenor says, and if Thalía has been taken, she's probably not the only one! So you all better rush home to check on your own kids and families!

Her voice ignited the room. The crowd roared back to life, not drunken laughter this time, but raw anger, united in purpose.

The storm had broken.

The hunt for Thalía had begun.

CHAPTER 22

The Warehouse of Shadows

Thalía...

The wagon screeched to a halt, the sudden jolt throwing Thalía against the wooden boards. Before she could gather her senses, the back of the carriage banged open and harsh voices barked at the captives.

"Out! All of you, move! Faster!"

Rough hands yanked the children by their arms and shoved them toward the ground. The men jeered and spat insults, their vulgar laughter cutting through the night.

"You stink like pigs!" one growled, shoving a boy so hard he nearly fell face-first.

"Keep your heads down! Don't you dare look at me!" another snapped. "You raise your eyes, and I'll break your teeth in."

Thalía stumbled forward with the others, her wrists bound tight, her bare feet stinging against gravel. She could see Marco's face in her mind, his smile, his hope, and clung to the thought of him as fear threatened to consume her.

At every chance, she quickly darted her eyes upward, desperate to confirm Marco hadn't been captured too. Each time she failed to spot him, a small breath of relief escaped her.

The children were herded to a wide warehouse door that groaned as it opened. A foul stench poured out—rust, mildew, sweat, and despair. But before they could enter, the traffickers lined them up.

"Clothes off," one ordered. His voice was low, mocking, final.

The kids froze, wide-eyed, confused. Some began crying, clutching at their rags. One little girl shook her head violently, refusing. She was met with a hard slap that knocked her to the ground.

"Undress!" the man bellowed again, his grin twisted.

Thalía's heart hammered in her chest. She didn't move at first, but the sting of a whip cracking near her feet jolted her into action. With trembling hands, she stripped off the dust-stained clothes she'd worn for days. Around her, sobs filled the night as children, too embarrassed and terrified, obeyed one by one. Their small piles of clothing were left scattered in the dirt like discarded skins.

Once stripped, the men drove them forward into a side chamber of the warehouse. Metal pipes hissed above, and before anyone could react, a torrent of chilling water blasted down from hoses. The spray struck like needles, piercing skin with relentless pressure. The children screamed and cried, huddling against one another as the water pounded them.

"Scrub 'em down!" one of the men laughed. Buckets of gritty powder, lime, and soap were flung at their shivering bodies, scouring their skin raw. The men mocked them as they coughed and choked, tears mixing with suds.

"We gotta clean you little rats up before the buyers see you!" another sneered.

Thalía bit down on her teeth, refusing to give them the satisfaction of hearing her scream. The cold left her trembling violently, her teeth chattering uncontrollably. Inside her mind, she kept whispering: *Don't break. Don't give them what they want.*

At last, the hoses shut off. Their skin felt raw, their bodies shaking, their dignity stripped away. They were each tossed a thin, shapeless gown and rough socks, the garments doing little to ward off the chill.

Then came the cages.

The children were driven toward towering iron enclosures welded into the floor. The doors screeched as they opened, and one by one the captives were shoved inside like cattle. The clang of the lock echoed like a sentence passed down from above.

Thalía's fingers curled around the cold bars as she peered into the dim warehouse beyond. Lanterns flickered, throwing shadows across stacks of crates, chains, and armed guards leaning lazily against the walls. From other cages nearby, wide eyes stared back at her; dozens of children and young women, silent and broken.

And at the far end of the room, João watched. His expression was calm, calculating, like a merchant appraising livestock. His lips curved into a cruel smile when his eyes found Thalía.

"A fighter," he murmured, almost to himself. "But veeery pretty! She'll fetch a high price."

Thalía's heart pounded, but she held his gaze, even as her knees trembled beneath her. The fear was real, but so was her fire. Somewhere inside, beneath the humiliation and despair, a voice urged her not to surrender.

She wrapped her hands tighter around the bars.

They will not break me.

Poor Little Poor Girl

CHAPTER 23

Marco's Coping

It had been three days now, and there was still no sign of Thalía. Marco, Jared, and Camilla were posting missing pictures of Thalía along the roads and at local businesses, just like the others. Marco could not fathom that his beloved cousin was now missing.

Marco was not taking it well, as he was only a 12-year-old kid who had already been through a lot. Now the only blood relative he had in this world had been taken from him. He thought back to when both of their parents were killed, and Thalía was there with him, possibly saving his life as well. They went through the same extreme trauma that bound them so tightly together emotionally. Being together helped them support each other and understand that they had to move forward with life. He knew that no one else would ever care for him like she did and that he cared for her the same way. To him, Thalía was more of a sister than a cousin; they even shared the same heterochromia.

He went into a depressed state and did not want to talk, eat, or be associated with anyone. Fortunately, Jared and Camilla understood and gave him time to cope with Thalía's disappearance.

* * *

A New Resolve...

Months had passed, and there was still no sign of Thalía nor Carlos. Jared and Camilla talked to Marco and encouraged him to move forward because he still had a life to live. Marco vowed to Jared and Camilla that he would find whoever took his cousin and would bring a wrath upon them.

He said he was suspicious that it was João because of what he had done to him. When he tried to snatch him in the saloon's restroom. He said Thalía had always been very suspicious of him anyway and really did not feel comfortable around him, nor did she like him at all.

Jared told Marco that he still needed him around the saloon to take care of his obligations because he had to support himself. They could not afford to support him just like before now that Thalía was gone because they still had kids of their own to support. Jared went on to say that he missed Thalía too, as she was a good girl, but he needed him to move forward.

Although a young man, Marco understood and told Jared he would comply and take care of his responsibilities at the saloon.

The next day, Marco was present at the saloon, but his work ethic was severely dragging, as he was always thinking about his cousin Thalía. He did not know if she was alive or dead, and it bothered him extremely.

Eleanor noticed Marco's attitude and walked over to comfort him. She told him to keep his faith that his cousin was alive and well and that they would meet up again. This brought Marco to tears as he wanted to believe what Eleanor was saying, but at the same time, his life had not been good, so he did not have high expectations.

Marco then went off in a frantic spell. He asked Eleanor why the police were not doing anything to find his cousin or any of the other people who had gone missing. He said that there had been a lot of suspicious activity around there for the longest time with people coming up missing, and no one had ever done anything about it. He frantically went on to say that if they had money, the police would be all over this matter. He said, "Because we are poor, nobody cares about us!"

Eleanor understood how upset Marco was, but she did not want to lie to him or taint his thoughts. After all, he was completely right about what he was saying and had every right to feel the way he did.

She opened up and told him, "Yes, you are right, Marco, but what are *you* going to do about it?" Marco paused for a few seconds, looked up at Eleanor, and said, "One day I'm going to have enough money and power, and I am going to change all of this!" Eleanor, with watery eyes, looked down at Marco and said, "That's the exact spirit and fierceness I wanted to see and hear from you!"

Eleanor took a deep sigh, gained her composure, and told Marco, "Hey, look outside. Those kids are playing fútbol, and it looks like Jared's kids are playing too." She whispered, "I know you are better than them, why don't you go out there and take some of your frustrations out in the game."

Marco displayed a big smile, something Eleanor had not seen from him in a while, and ran outside to participate in the fútbol game.

* * *

A Vicious Game...

As Eleanor, Jared, and Camilla watched, Marco played the game of his life, filled with nothing but determination, frustration, and motivation. He dribbled through other kids much older than him, consistently scoring on the goalie who was much older than him, and leading his team to victory.

Toward the end of the game, one of the older guys tried to slow down Marco by doing a vicious slide tackle. Marco somehow managed to avoid getting seriously injured but took a nasty fall and bruised his side.

Marco got up in frustration and attacked the older guy who was almost twice his size. Normally, he wouldn't have to do that because Thalía would be there to have his back. But this time, it was only him. He punched the guy in the nose, and the older guy got up and punched him back. They started to tussle, and Eleanor shouted out for him to do the moves that she had taught him and Thalía.

He did the move and took advantage of the guy, taking him to the ground. He punched the guy a couple more times in the face and made his nose bleed.

At the same time, the parents were running toward both kids to break up the fight. As they were breaking them up, the parent who grabbed Marco held his hands to his side, and while he was defenseless, the older guy kicked Marco in the chest, knocking the wind out of him.

Marco stood up for himself against a bigger opponent and held his own. From that point on, none of the other guys attempted to fight him. Instead, they welcomed him to be on their team as he had proven to be a very good fútbol player and a scrappy little guy.

Eleanor, Camilla, and Jared all looked at each other after the event, holding back their smiles. Eleanor said, "Well, this was quite entertaining!" Jared said, "I think we've got ourselves a little fútbol player here!" Camilla says, "and a little boxer!" They all laughed out loud and walked back into the saloon with Marco.

CHAPTER 24

The Wall of Faces

Thalía...

The two guards moved toward a wall plastered with photographs. Thalía's eyes followed them from the shadows of her cage, heart pounding in her chest. As the guards inspected the images, her stomach churned in horror.

There were pictures of most all the people in the warehouse, and many others she recognized from her village, missing for months. Her gaze slowly drifted to the corner of the wall. There it was: her own photo, that was taken by João himself. Everything clicked. The smiling "photographer" at the saloon had been plotting this all along, documenting each victim for future capture.

The guards turned back to the cages. One of them held her photo in his hand, turning it over, smirking.

"Damn," he said with a leering laugh, "I'd like to keep this one for myself!"

The other chuckled and added, "Boss will kill us if we damage the goods."

Thalía shrank back, trying to make herself invisible, but the guard stepped closer, holding the photo up.

"Hey, hey, pretty girl! What's your name?" he demanded, voice low and taunting.

She muttered softly, "Thalía..."

"I can't hear you!" he snapped. "What's your damn name?"

Knowing she was forbidden to look directly at them, she kept her head down, louder this time: "Thalía."

"Look at me when I'm talking to you, little bitch!" "I want to see that pretty face live and in-person," he barked, thrusting the photo into her line of sight. When she glanced up, he frowned. "What the hell happened to your eyes?! They don't look like that in this picture."

Thalía blinked, confused. Then she remembered—the chaos, the assaults, the cold water hoses, and realized her eye contact had been knocked out. In a soft, hesitant voice, she replied, "I... I have heterochromia. My eyes are different colors naturally."

The guard scowled, disbelief twisting his face. "What the hell is that? Don't try to use big words to confuse me."

"I... I'm not trying to confuse you," Thalía stammered. "It's the medical term. I wear a single contact so my eyes would match."

The guard's face darkened, anger flashing. "Huh. Weird." He muttered something under his breath and stormed off toward João, who had been watching from across the room.

João's eyes blazed as he strode up to Thalía, grabbing her shoulders. "Why didn't you tell me this before?" he demanded. Thalía froze, unable to speak, only able to cry as her body shook with fear.

"Find her another eye contact!" João barked to a female worker, voice sharp as a whip. He studied Thalía's face, scrutinizing the mismatched eyes. "Stop! Wait," he said suddenly, tilting his head. "A light-gray contact… that will match. It'll make her even more… attractive in an exotic way; MONEY!"

The nurse scurried into the nearest town, returning after a while with contacts, but none were exact. "I'm sorry," she said, "we couldn't match the shade. It's unique."

João's grin twisted into fury. He snatched the contacts from her hands, pushing her to the floor. "Incompetent!" he barked. "Pick yourself up!" The worker stayed down as she was afraid he would knock her down again.

Thalía's hands trembled as she was directed to put in the light-gray contact. When she did, João studied her for a long, chilling moment, then smiled with satisfaction. "Yes… now she is even more marketable."

His gaze shifted back to the female worker still lying on the floor. João walked by her, kicked her in the rear, and spat, "Get up! Feed these damn kids! Prepare them!"

Thalía's heart raced. She pressed herself against the cold bars of the cage, fighting the terror threatening to consume her. Around her, the other children shuffled, trembling, realizing with sinking dread the grim fate that awaited them, and that João's twisted control was absolute.

CHAPTER 25

The Auction

The children were fed meager slop for nourishment, their stomachs still unsettled from fear and exhaustion. Two older women moved among them, brushing their hair, straightening their clothes, and fussing over them as if preparing them for some type of grotesque event.

João strode through the warehouse, his black hat casting a shadow over his face, and sneered at the kids. "See?" he said with a mocking tone, "I told you, you'll be better off with us. We clean you, clothe you, feed you, and give you a place to sleep." He paused, then walked off, his signature laugh echoing through the warehouse.

The next morning, the sunlight poured through the sliding doors of the warehouse as it creaked open. João appeared at the entrance, flanked by twenty men and three women dressed in fine, elegant clothing. His voice boomed: "Let the games begin!"

Thalía's heart sank. As her eyes scanned the crowd, the terrible truth hit her: she was now part of a sex-trafficking ring. Her mind raced, piecing together the disappearances of women and children from neighboring villages. Every missing person she had heard about, every suspicious story, it was all real, and she was now one of the victims. Thalía feels like she cannot catch a break as she feels she is always the poor and unlucky girl.

The bidding process began. The rich clients murmured amongst themselves, calculating their offers. João directed the children onto a raised platform, parading them in front of the buyers. The first to be displayed was a girl who looked to be about sixteen. João commanded her to remove her robe, leaving her stark naked.

Humiliation and fear washed over her. A single tear rolled down her cheek, and João smacked her roughly. "Don't cry!" he barked. "The rest of you," he warned, "if I see a single tear, you'll get the same treatment."

One of the women buyers spoke sharply. "Don't damage the goods, João, or you'll decrease their value."

João's demeanor softened, and he nodded respectfully. "Of course. We wouldn't want to devalue them," he said, turning his gaze toward the other children. His eyes pierced them with silent warning; they shivered, understanding exactly what he meant.

As the process continued, Thalía was called to the platform fifth. Her heart raced, but she kept her composure. She forced herself to stand tall, refusing to show the humiliation and fear boiling inside her. She would not give him the satisfaction.

The bidding for Thalía quickly escalated. The wealthy buyers recognized her value immediately, and the numbers soared. Finally, a male-female couple won the bid: the same woman who had scolded João for hitting the first girl. Thalía felt a flicker of relief. Perhaps, in this nightmare, these were the least cruel buyers.

The couple introduced themselves as Hugo and Maria. They spoke gently, offering Thalía words of comfort. "You'll be fine," Maria said softly. "Just follow our rules, and you'll be safe." Despite their involvement in this illegal business, their demeanor seemed calm, almost kind, and for a brief moment, Thalía allowed herself to hope.

Alongside Thalía, the couple had also purchased a boy named Ramon, fifteen years old, about a year older than her. Thalía couldn't help but be reminded of her cousin Marco. Maria smiled and told her, "You'll get to know Ramon well. You can look out for each other."

Thalía's stomach churned with fear and uncertainty, but amidst the terror, she resolved to stay strong. She had endured much already, and she would endure this too.

CHAPTER 26

The Estate

When they arrived at Hugo and Maria's estate, Thalía and Ramon were struck by the size and luxury of the property. The house was well-groomed, surrounded by manicured gardens, and dozens of workers moved about, maids, groundskeepers, and cooks, keeping everything in pristine order.

Hugo and Maria led them through the house, explaining the rules in a tone that was calm but chilling. They explained that there is nothing around this area for miles except for wooden areas. Then they said something that terrified them both. "If you ever try to escape, our guards and vicious dogs will hunt you down, shoot, and kill you in your tracks. You won't make it out alive," Hugo said, his eyes hard. Maria added, "Stay close to the house, follow instructions, and you'll be safe." Both kids felt a knot tighten in their stomachs. The danger was real, and the couple's words made it clear they were trapped.

* * *

New Living Arrangements...

They were shown to the basement, where two small rooms had been prepared. Each had a single bed, a nightstand, a small sink, and a barred window that let in little light. The basement felt cold and oppressive, and the kids realized they would be under constant supervision.

For the next three weeks, nothing overtly threatening happened. Thalía and Ramon helped with cleaning, cooking, and yard work. The couple treated them well enough to avoid suspicion, meals were provided, and they were clothed and safe, but the kids remained on edge. Every sound from upstairs, every command from a worker, reminded them that they were not free.

Thalía's thoughts often drifted to her cousin Marco and the saloon. She cried at night, missing her home and her family, and felt trapped in a gilded cage. Ramon, quiet and observant, seemed equally aware that they were only a step away from danger.

* * *

A Suspicious Celebration...

About six weeks in, the estate became a flurry of activity. Workers were decorating, hanging lights, and preparing tables. Thalía and Ramon watched from the basement windows, unsure what was happening. "Maybe it's a celebration?" Ramon whispered. Thalía shook her head. "With Hugo and Maria, I doubt it's that simple."

That evening, the party began. Guests arrived in fancy cars, dressed in elegant attire. Music blared, and the estate was filled with laughter and conversation. From their vantage point, Thalía and Ramon saw that the adults were indulging and pleasuring themselves sexually in ways that no young child should witness. They were clearly in charge of the household, and the estate operated under strict hierarchies.

* * *

A Test of Compliance...

A knock at the basement door made Thalía jump. One of the lady workers entered, carrying a clipboard. She threw Thalía some erotic-looking clothes, and told her to put it on. Thalía immediately got concerned because she was fearful of what this was all about. "You need to come upstairs," she said, her voice low. "Just follow the rules, and no one will get hurt. Tears immediately started rolling down Thalía's face, fearful of what was about to happen next. Do what you're told, and you'll be fine." The lady said.

The lady told her again that she just needed to do what they were about to tell her because if she didn't, it would not turn out well for her. She then went on to tell her that she was once in her spot, so she knew exactly what she was going through. She stressed for her to be strong and just go with the flow so she doesn't get hurt.

Thalía now realized that all the workers on the estate were probably forced to do the same things she was about to do. That they were never able to escape and, therefore, turned into other types of assets for Hugo and Maria. She figured this was her life now, so there was no use in fighting it.

The lady then escorted Thalía to this big open room that had only a bed mattress in the middle of the floor. As she approached, she saw someone on the bed who was pretty much naked. It was Ramon. He had a horrified look on his face, as he did not know what was about to happen. When he saw Thalía approaching, he understood what they wanted them to do.

Thalía also now understood that her role was to have intercourse with Ramon in front of all these other grown men and women. They were all horseshoe-shaped around the bed, laughing, drinking, smoking, and doing drugs, and excited and anticipating what they were about to witness. Most of them were naked and ready to have sexual relations with anyone they wanted in the room. They tossed a few sex toys at them and made them use them on each other. Then laughed when the two didn't know, or were confused on how to use them.

Both Thalía and Ramon were frightened, the wiped each others tears from running down their faces, but they both knew what they must do or else. Thalía hugged Ramon in comfort and whispered in his ear what the lady told her. Reluctantly, they performed the acts that their owners wanted them to do while the other grown people in the room watched and pleasured themselves. They both felt humiliated by the event but also knew this was not going to be the last time they would have to do this.

* * *

Reflection and Resolve...

As they returned to the basement that night, exhausted and humiliated, Thalía whispered to Ramon, "We have to figure out a way out of here. We can't stay trapped forever." Ramon nodded silently. Though the danger was real, and the adults around them were ruthless, a spark of determination grew in them both.

They didn't know when or how, but Thalía and Ramon began to plan their escape. For now, survival was their top priority, and every day would be a careful balance of obedience and observation.

CHAPTER 27

Breaking Point

The next day, Hugo and Maria carried on as if nothing had happened. They smiled at Thalía and Ramon, telling them they had "done well" and would be rewarded. But the reward was nothing they had hoped for.

Over time, the tasks Hugo and Maria demanded became more grueling and psychologically taxing. Throughout the year, they made Thalía and Ramon perform these unspeakable acts on a routine basis. It even got to the point where they made them do special, weird requests and unfathomable acts to each other to satisfy their sick pleasures.

As months passed, Thalía realized she could no longer endure the constant abuse. Ramon, however, had a young, weak mind and actually started enjoying the acts. He was so brainwashed that his mind adapted to their harsh control, and he began to accept the rules unquestioningly. He no longer understood what was right or wrong.

One day, when Thalía refused to follow a particularly cruel order, Hugo and Maria made an example of her. She was confined to a small, dark room in the basement with limited access to food and water for several days. The isolation weighed heavily on her, but it also steeled her resolve.

The lady who had once warned Thalía before came quietly into the room. She led Thalía down the hall and opened a door to reveal another girl, beaten, exhausted, and frightened, who had been punished for defiance. "This is what happens when you don't obey," she whispered. "They control people by fear... She said this girl was also injected with drugs to make her dependent on them so they could control her. This was indeed a shock, and Thalía did not want to end up like that.

The sight was horrifying, but it strengthened Thalía's determination. She refused to let herself become broken or controlled completely.

Hugo and Maria, seeing her defiance, began to consider her a problem. They whispered about selling or moving her to another location—someone else's responsibility, someone else's problem.

Because of Thalía's beauty, they figured they could offer a trade or resell her to someone else and get a hefty return. For this reason, addicting her to drugs will not be the best approached, as she may then be considered damaged goods.

Thalía realized she had to act. She couldn't wait for them to decide her fate. If she wanted to survive, and maybe even escape, she would have to take matters into her own hands.

CHAPTER 28

The Capture

The next day brought another significant turn in Thalía's journey. Late at night, Hugo crept into Thalía's room, claiming he had come to "help" her after her confinement. He unlocked the doors and told her she could shower and prepare for the day ahead. Thalía, wary and on edge, complied, unsure of his intentions.

As she showered, she realized he wasn't acting as usual. His behavior was controlling and manipulative, and her instincts screamed that something was wrong. Drawing on the self-defense techniques she had secretly learned from Eleanor back at the saloon, Thalía braced herself. She stayed alert, positioning herself near the door, ready to fight if necessary.

Suddenly, Hugo made a move toward her in an attempt to rape her. He underestimated Thalía's small size for weakness. Thalía immediately defended herself, using her training to push him back, kick, and create distance. Her shouts alerted Ramon in the next room, as well as some of the other workers in the house.

Maria, hearing the commotion, stormed down the hall urgently. But instead of blaming Hugo, her jealousy and temper made her direct her anger at Thalía, seeing her as a threat and a problem to control. Maria warned Thalía in a cold, icy tone: "You're going to regret this... you won't get away from what's coming next."

The very next morning, as the sun rose, Ramon noticed movement outside the small basement window. A truck had pulled up, and men were conversing with Maria. The tension in the air was palpable. Thalía and Ramon knew something bad was about to happen.

Before Thalía could react, two men burst into the basement. Despite her struggles and attempts to resist, she was overpowered and forced into the back of the truck. The vehicle roared to life and sped off into the woods. Ramon, left alone in the room, realized grimly that she had been singled out, what awaited her now may be dangerous, and he could only hope she would survive.

CHAPTER 29

Welcome to the U.S.

In a too-familiar scene, Thalía awoke in the back of a truck alongside a lot of other kids and women, en route to an unknown destination. The only difference was that this time, some were tied and bound, while others were not. She didn't understand why, but she knew she did not want to be there.

Since she figured it would be just like the last time, she did not say or do anything that might cause her harm or suspicion. She just sat back, went along for the ride, and waited to see what would happen next.

* * *

A Long Journey...

After a long, excruciating ride that seemed like an eternity, she and the others were instructed to exit the truck. The doors opened after a period of complete darkness, and the world outside seemed to have grown immensely. Some of the people were directed to link up with others who were already waiting for them as if they knew each other. Others were directed to yet another truck to unknown destinations. She saw money being handed over to the guys who had transported them, along with hugs and kisses. On the other hand, some of the other people were pouting and crying against their will, including her.

Looking back at the container, Thalía realized the truth: she hadn't been in a truck at all. She had been shipped, literally shipped, to another country. Her body trembled at the thought. She guessed she may have been unconscious until they had transported her from the initial truck into the shipping container.

She also now understood that some of the people in the shipping container had been brought to this new country to join their family members, while others, like her, were being forced into other activities against their will.

Thalía was now in a foreign country she knew she had never been to before. Everything looked so different to her. All she could think about was an opportunity to escape. Although at the moment she was too ill and weak, she had to wait until she could build up some strength.

* * *

Auction Day...

Going through a similar process as the first time, Thalía pretty much knew the routine when they got out of the truck and into the warehouse. The new location was very familiar with the other processes she had gone through in Honduras. They took everyone into a building, got them cleaned up, fed them, and prepared them for sale. This process took longer this time because they wanted to make everyone look healthy before the buyers came in for the sale.

Throughout this whole ordeal, all Thalía could think about was escaping so that she could reunite with her cousin Marco. Approximately five days elapsed, and nothing significant had happened yet. Thalía still did not know where she was, but she did, however, hear people speaking English here and there. She remembered that as a younger girl, her father had always spoken about going to the United States, so he spoke his broken English to her from time to time. She had refined her English by working at the saloon, as it was necessary due to the different nationalities of people coming there. Lastly, she and Marco used to practice together while practicing the self-defense moves that Eleanor had taught them.

The auction day arrived, and Thalía was highly sought after because of her beauty that had been circulated in the black market. When her turn came, the bidding was fierce. Finally, she was sold to an older Arabic man named **Hamza**, who instructed the sellers to take special care of her. She was "too valuable" to damage. He told the seller that he would be sending one of his own men to transport her to him. She was to be flown privately to Saudi Arabia. He said she was a beauty meant only for him, which is why he paid the highest amount he had ever paid for a woman.

* * *

A Twist of Fate...

Hamza's men arrived in the U.S. to get Thalía. He went through the process with the seller, and because of the emphasis placed on her by the Arabic owner, Thalía was given preferential treatment. They were in a private vehicle headed to the airstrip, as she was scheduled to be transported overseas via private jet to avoid detection. However, all of a sudden the car jolted. A flat tire. The driver cursed under his breath, pulling to the side of the highway.

As they were stopped, a couple of thugs driving by saw the nice vehicle on the side of the road and decided to seize the opportunity to rob them. They swerved off at the first exit, circled back onto the road, and tailed the car Thalía was in. Their battered sedan rattled up close, belching thick black smoke from the tailpipe as they slid in behind the sleek, polished ride. Pulling to a stop, they climbed out, masking their intent with fake concern as they approached the driver, acting as though they'd come to help. The driver told them, "Thanks for offering to assist, but we don't need your help. Besides, we already have someone en route to help us."

The thug took offense at the way the driver talked to him and caused a dramatic scene, repeating in a condescending tone, "Oh, you don't need our help? Oh, you don't need the help from our kind? Well, it looks to me like you do. You got a flat and you can't go anywhere because you're too clean and uppity to change the tire!"

One of the thugs looked through the back window and saw Thalía, realizing that her hands were bound. He thought it was a little weird but didn't really care. Thalía looked at him in his eyes, and he saw how pretty her eyes and face were, so at that moment, he decided he wanted her, and he was going to take her.

The first thug signaled to his partner that it was time. They swiftly pulled out their guns and shot the driver. The Arabic transporter jumped out with his gun, but the other thug's partner shot him! Now it was only Thalía, who was extremely scared and did not know what was going on. He grabbed Thalía out of the car with her hands still bound and asked her, "What the fuck kinda freaky shit y'all got going on up in here?!" but proceeded to take her to his car.

Although Thalía was afraid, she was still thinking that this could be her opportunity to escape. She struggled slightly, but she still went along with the thugs. She figured she stood a better chance of getting away from them than these professionals in the sex-trafficking ring. The other thug went through the pockets and vehicle of the driver and the Arabic escort and took their jewelry, money, and anything valuable he could find. They got into the car and sped off with Thalía.

The thug was driving fast to get away from the scene of the crime as quickly as possible. As they drove, they were both laughing, drinking, and bragging about how much valuables and money they got from the robbery. The one in the backseat with Thalía boasted to her about how much fun they were going to have with her when they get back to their hotel room. Thalía did not know whether to be scared or grateful. She just sat back and blanked her mind to everything that was going on. Everything was happening so fast; it was so scary, and she did not know what to do.

All of a sudden, things slowed down as she looked up at a road sign that said, "Welcome to Miami." She now realized that she was in the United States. She had to get away as soon as possible because someone here should definitely be able to help her.

The thugs in the car were still carrying on, drinking, and talking about the robbery, so she just remained calm as she figured out her game plan. They got to the hotel, and the guys took her in, excited about how pretty she was and what a great catch they had made. They took her inside, bragging about her beauty, pawing at her, certain they had just hit the jackpot.

Thalía understood what was about to happen because she had been in this situation before. She figured she just needed to keep them drinking so that they would pass out, and then she could get away. As the night went on, the thugs were playing music, drinking, being touchy-feely with her, making her kiss them, and violating her personal space. As the night went on, one of the thugs drank so much that he passed out, which was definitely her plan. The other one was lying on the bed and made her lay under his arm and massage his genitals. He seemed to doze in and out, falling asleep. She saw an opportunity to escape, so she slowly slid from under his arm.

When she tried, it stirred him awake, and anger flared as he realized she was attempting to slip away. He yanked her back inside, throwing her onto the bed before demanding to know why she was running and acting ungrateful after they had 'rescued' her. Thalía, thinking quickly, softened her tone and said she only wanted a bit of fresh air, that he needn't worry because she truly was grateful... and she was going to prove just how grateful she could be. She told him to pull down his pants, she proceeded to please him until he released, then slowly lowered him back on the bed. At this point, he was so drunk and relieved, he fell right back to sleep.

The other guy was still asleep on the bed and never even woke up.

The room was filled with their snores. Outside, cars honked and roared along the main road. They didn't stir. This was her moment. Quiet as a shadow, Thalía slipped from the bed, gathered herself, and crept out the door.

She was now free but had nowhere to go. Warm breezy night air hit her face as she stumbled down the street, her legs weak but her spirit on fire.

She took in the unfamiliar surroundings—towering buildings, flashing lights, neon signs blazing in every direction. It felt surreal, as if she'd stumbled into a beautiful nightmare.

After wandering around the city for what seemed like hours, she finally ducked into a narrow alley, collapsed beside a trash can, and let exhaustion take her.

The chains that had held her so long were gone, at last. She wasn't on a boat or in a container. She was in the United States, and that meant there was still hope.

CHAPTER 30

A Chance Encounter

At sunrise, Cynthia, the owner of a small local diner, stepped out the back door to toss a bag of trash into the alley dumpster. The morning air hit her face, and that's when she noticed a small figure curled up beside the garbage can. For a split second, Cynthia thought it might be another body left in the alley—something she had sadly seen before.

She set the trash down and knelt beside the girl. Gently, she shook her shoulder.

"Hey… hey, sweetheart, you alive?"

Thalía's eyes flew open wide. She recoiled, trembling with fear, her breathing sharp and shallow.

Cynthia raised her hands in a calming gesture. "It's okay, honey. I'm not gonna hurt you. What are you doing out here? Do you need help?"

Thalía didn't speak. Her face tightened with suspicion and fear, but she gave a few small nods.

Cynthia softened her voice. "Why don't you come inside? I'll fix you a hot cup of tea. You look like you could use something warm."

After a long pause, Thalía rose shakily to her feet. She followed Cynthia inside, still tense and wary, her movements stiff as if she expected a trap at any moment.

Cynthia sat her at the counter and poured steaming tea into a chipped mug. From the bruises and the guarded way the girl carried herself, Cynthia could tell this young one had been through something.

As Thalía sipped the tea, Cynthia slipped quietly into the back room and dialed the police, whispering about the girl she had found in her alley. She hoped she was doing the right thing.

Back at the counter, Thalía's eyes locked on the television. A breaking news bulletin blared: *Two men found dead on the highway, an apparent robbery gone wrong.* Images of the wrecked luxury car flashed on-screen, followed by photos of the two victims: the Arabic driver and escort.

Thalía's stomach dropped. A wave of relief hit her, at least they couldn't hurt her now, but it was tangled with dread. She had been there. She had been in that car. What if someone blamed her? What happens when the two thugs wake up and come looking for her?

Cynthia returned, glanced at the TV, and shook her head. "That's a damn shame," she muttered. She turned back to Thalía, her voice gentle. "Sweetheart, is there anything I can do for you? Anything at all?"

Thalía just stared into her cup.

Trying another approach, Cynthia sighed and said, "I've got a daughter, her name isCheney. About your age. She's had a hard life too. Always out there, always in danger... I'm scared to death every time she leaves the house. I just want her to come back home so I can keep her safe. This diner, " she gestured around ", it's nothing fancy. But it pays the bills. And if she'd just stay, I could protect her. After a pause (she mumbled to herself), I know I could've done better by her." Her voice cracked with guilt.

Thalía studied her face. She saw genuine hurt in Cynthia's eyes. Slowly, in broken English, she whispered, "I… I worked… place like this. Makes me think of home."

Cynthia leaned forward, surprised. "Where are you from?"

Thalía opened her mouth, but before she could answer, the screech of sirens cut through the morning quiet. Two police cars skidded to a stop outside the diner.

Thalía's heart sank. She knew there was no running now.

The officers entered, and Cynthia quickly raised her hands in apology. "I'm sorry, sweetheart," she said softly to Thalía. "But I can see you need help, and that's what I'm trying to get you. Please don't be angry. I hope you understand." Her voice broke as she added, "I wish I'd done this for my own daughter."

Thalía searched her face. Cynthia's sincerity was undeniable.

As the police began asking questions, the news report replayed on the diner's TV. The words *murder suspects still at large* scrolled across the screen. Thalía's mind raced. This was her chance.

"I… I know where they are," she blurted out.

Both officers froze. "You *know* where the killers are?" one asked.

Thalía nodded quickly. "Hotel… close. They there."

The policemen exchanged a glance. "Show us," one said firmly. "You won't have to go inside. You can stay in the car."

Thalía hesitated, but then nodded. If those men were locked away, they couldn't come after her.

111

Minutes later, the squad cars pulled into the dingy hotel parking lot less than five minutes from the diner. Just as Thalía had hoped, the thugs were still there, passed out drunk, sprawled across the bed.

The police stormed the room, weapons drawn. Within moments, both men were cuffed and dragged out. In the room, officers found everything they needed: jewelry, cash, and the murder weapon.

As the thugs were shoved into the back of the squad car, Thalía sat in silence. She wasn't free yet, not by a long shot, but the chains on her life now felt just a little bit looser.

CHAPTER 31

Where Is My Product?

When word reached Hamza about what had happened—the robbery, the murder of his men, and worst of all, Thalía's disappearance, his fury boiled over. The loss of his men meant nothing compared to the humiliation of losing what he had paid dearly for.

He slammed his fist against the table, rattling the glassware.

"Where is my product?" he roared over the phone to the trafficker who had sold her. "I don't care what happened on your pathetic streets. If I do not have the girl in my possession soon, you will be swimming with the fishes!"

The seller stammered, trying to defend himself. "Hamza, please, you must understand. It wasn't my fault. I did everything I could! Your men were ambushed and killed by some random asshole thugs, they were—"

"I don't want excuses!" Hamza cut him off, his voice cold and lethal. "You think I paid the highest price for excuses? I paid your top American dollar for *her, a*nd now I'm just supposed to accept that "POOF", she is gone?! I'm sending four men this time! If you don't have her ready for transport when my men arrive, you will regret the day you were born."

The line went dead.

The seller stood frozen, the phone still pressed to his ear. He knew Hamza's threats were not empty words. The man had money, reach, and men who would carve him apart without hesitation. If he failed, torture, or worse, awaited him.

Panicked, the seller barked orders at his crew.

"Get out there and find that girl! Search every alley, every motel, every street corner if you have to. I don't care how long it takes, bring her back to me alive. Do you hear me? Alive!"

The goons scattered, but deep down the seller knew the truth: recovering Thalía would not be easy. She had already slipped through professional hands once. She was resourceful, stronger than she looked, and desperate enough to risk everything for freedom.

And every hour she stayed hidden, Hamza's wrath grew closer.

CHAPTER 32

A Dangerous Intersection

Thalía sat in the corner of the small interrogation room, her hands folded tightly in her lap. She hadn't been arrested, but the police wanted answers. Two detectives stood over her, trying to balance sympathy with suspicion.

"You're lucky to be alive," one of them said, sliding a cup of water toward her. "But we need to know the truth. Why were you in that car? Who are you running from?"

Thalía lowered her eyes, struggling with the English words. "I… not bad girl. They… they take me. I no want to go." Her voice trembled, but her gaze was steady, pleading for them to believe her.

The younger detective leaned forward. "Okay, okay. You're saying you were kidnapped?"

Thalía nodded quickly, tears brimming. "Yes. Please… no send me back. They come for me."

The older detective exchanged a glance with his partner. He had seen fear like this before, and he knew it wasn't an act. "She's telling the truth," he muttered. "And if she's right, whoever's after her isn't done yet."

Outside the station, Cynthia paced anxiously. She had insisted on coming along, worried sick for the girl she had found in the alley.

Watching Thalía shake and cry under the fluorescent lights broke her heart. She thought again of her own daughter, Cheney, and whispered to herself, *I couldn't save you... but maybe I can save her.*

* * *

Meanwhile. . . At the Miami International Airport

The private jet touched down smoothly, and two tall men in dark suits walked briskly through the terminal with diplomatic-style bags slung over their shoulders. They looked like businessmen, but their eyes told a darker story.

Hamza's enforcers had arrived.

One of them lit a cigarette as soon as they stepped outside into the humid Florida air. "We find her fast. Hamza's patience is gone."

His partner smirked. "And what about the seller?"

The first man's expression hardened. "Dead man walking. But first, we take the girl."

They slid into a sleek black SUV waiting at the curb, engines humming as they sped toward the city.

* * *

Back at the station...

The detectives were discussing placing Thalía into protective custody. "If what she's saying checks out," the younger one said, "she's a witness in a homicide case, maybe even tied to an international trafficking ring. She's not safe out there."

Thalía overheard the words *not safe* and felt a shiver run down her spine. She looked up and whispered, "They come... they always come."

She was right.

Even as she sat under the harsh fluorescent lights, the men sent to reclaim her were already less than an hour away, drawing closer with every mile.

CHAPTER 33

Marco's Waiver

Marco... (meanwhile, in Honduras)

Marco sat at the table in the back of the saloon, staring blankly into his drink. The laughter of the crowd, the clinking of glasses, even the music from the piano in the corner felt distant. His thoughts kept circling back to Thalía.

It had been months. Too many months. And there had been no word, no sighting, no trace of her. Each passing day weighed heavier on his chest.

Jared noticed the slump in his shoulders. Eleanor, polishing glasses behind the counter, caught the look in Marco's eyes. Camila too, sitting close by, felt his sadness pressing into the room.

Finally, Marco muttered, almost to himself, "Maybe I'll never see her again." His voice cracked with the words.

Eleanor set the glass down gently and came around the counter. "Marco," she said softly, placing a hand on his shoulder, "you don't know that. She's strong. Just like you. Wherever she is, you keep her alive in here." She tapped a finger against his chest.

Jared chimed in, steady as ever. "Life doesn't stop, son. You keep living, you keep fighting. That's how you honor her."

Camila leaned in with her gentle smile. "And as long as you keep the faith, Marco, she'll always be with you. Always."

Marco swallowed hard, trying to push down the lump in his throat. He nodded. "I'll never stop looking for her. I promise. But... I'll keep moving forward too. I have to."

And he did.

Marco threw himself into the makeshift school during the day, learning fast and earning respect from his teachers. At night, he worked hard in the saloon, taking on responsibilities and growing sharper under Jared's guidance. But the place he shined the brightest was on the field.

Fútbol became his outlet. His body had changed, he'd shot up taller than many of the grown men in town, his legs powerful, his stride unstoppable. Against the older players, he was a force. People whispered about him around town: *that boy Marco, he's is something special.*

One hot afternoon, Marco was tearing through defenders during a community game when a stranger stopped to watch. Felipe, with his bottle of soda in hand, stood at the fence in awe. He hadn't seen raw talent like this in years.

When the game ended, Felipe approached, clapping his hands. "Hey, kid! That was incredible. You ever thought about playing on a real team?"

Marco wiped sweat from his brow. "I... I don't have money for that. And I'd need permission from my guardians."

Felipe grinned. "Don't worry about money. I've got a semi-pro team, and I think you'd fit right in. In fact, I need a forward, one of my starters just went down with a hamstring injury. If you want, I can speak with your guardian."

Marco's eyes lit up with hope. "Oh yes, please do. His name is Jared and you can find him at the Saloon in the villiage.."

That evening, Felipe sat across from Jared at a saloon table, explaining his pitch. Camila stood nearby with her arms crossed, watching carefully. Eleanor listened from behind the counter, polishing another glass but not missing a word.

"Look, Mr. Jared," Felipe began, "this kid is something rare and special. I run a semi-pro team, and we've got a big match coming up. I want Marco in that lineup. I'll pay all the fees, cover transport, even arrange rides to practice and games. You won't have to lift a finger."

Jared studied him carefully. "You heard about all these kids going missing lately?"

Felipe nodded grimly. "Yes. Some of the female players from a different teams vanished a few months ago. Terrible! But we've increased security like never before, security escorts, strict check-ins, background checks on every adult. We've tightened everything. He'd be safe with us, I give you my word."

Marco leaned forward, eyes shining. "Please, Jared. This is my chance. I can do this."

Jared scratched his chin. "He also helps me with the saloon. fútbol takes time. That's money out of my pocket."

Felipe raised a hand, smiling. "It's semi-pro, Marco would earn a small salary, but should be much more than what her is making here. He can still contribute, while earning for himself."

At that, Camila and Eleanor exchanged a look. Eleanor raised an eyebrow and Camila gave a subtle nod. Jared read their faces like an open book.

"Alright," Jared sighed. "What's the catch?"

Felipe pulled out some papers. "Only thing, we need to talk about his age. Marco, how old are you?"

"Thirteen," Marco said proudly.

Felipe couldn't hold onto the pen as it dropped to the floor—his face turned pale. "Thirteen?! Dios mío, I thought you were much older than that! In this league, minimum age is sixteen. Only way around it is… Jared, you'd have to sign a waiver, and I'm not even sure if that would work"

Marco turned to Jared, his face full of pleading. "Please. I can handle it. I know I can."

Jared stared at him for a long moment, then slowly nodded. "No doubt about it." He signed the paper.

Eleanor shook her head with a smile, and Camila let out a breath of relief.

After the paperwork, Eleanor pulled Marco aside. She lowered her voice so only he could hear. "Marco, you remember the fire in your eyes when you thought about Thalía? That same energy, you put it into your game. Channel it. Let it push you forward. Don't let the anger destroy you. Let it make you unstoppable."

Marco nodded firmly.

Eleanor turned to Felipe. "And when everything works out, maybe he'll earn enough to do more than just play fútbol. Maybe he'll find a way to fight poverty… and find his cousin."

Felipe gave a slow, respectful nod. "Then let's make it happen."

Marco felt something powerful stirring inside him. HOPE!

CHAPTER 34

Into the U.S. System

Thalía...

After the chaos with the murders, Thalía was finally in police custody. She was exhausted, bruised, and wary, but safe, for now.

The officers began asking her the standard questions: name, age, place of residence. With no other choice, she told them everything; her abduction, the trafficking, Hugo and Maria, the shipment overseas, and the horrifying events that led up to her escape. Her voice shook at times, but she spoke with as much clarity as she could muster.

The officers listened, horrified. It was immediately clear that Thalía was underage and could not be released back into the streets. They contacted a social worker, explained the situation, and began processing her into the U.S. system.

Thalía was placed in a temporary children's group home while arrangements were made for her long-term care. The facility was already overcrowded, so staff had to shuffle kids around to make space for her. It wasn't ideal—beds were tight, rooms loud, and the meals weren't particularly appetizing, but Thalía was grateful. After months of uncertainty, she finally had a roof over her head, warmth, and regular meals.

Despite the relative safety, Thalía kept to herself. She spoke to no one more than necessary, avoided drawing attention, and spent hours thinking about her cousin Marco. She longed to return home, to be with him, to see the familiar faces and places that had once brought her comfort.

But the group home was busy, and with so many children, her case received only limited attention. The process to determine her next steps, whether to return to her country or be placed in another temporary home, seemed to drag endlessly. Days turned into weeks, and weeks into months, leaving Thalía frustrated and increasingly impatient.

Four months had passed. Thalía was still waiting, still uncertain of her future. Her frustration finally boiled over when another girl at the home began teasing her relentlessly. Thalía tried to ignore her at first, but when the taunts persisted, she snapped. A scuffle broke out, and by the end of it, Thalía had given the girl a black eye.

The incident left Thalía shaken, angry at herself for losing control, but also fueled by a simmering rage at the slow-moving system that kept her trapped far from home and her beloved cousin.

For Thalía, this was only the beginning. If she couldn't wait for the system to help her, she would have to find another way.

CHAPTER 35

A Fresh Start

Fortunately for Thalía, after the fight at the group home, a married couple, Mr. and Mrs. Neymore, a white male and a Hispanic female arrived looking to foster a child. Out of all the kids, they chose Thalía. Her ability to speak Spanish resonated with them, and they felt it would help their daughter, Rachel, who was about Thalía's age. Naturally, this sparked jealousy among the other girls, but Thalía didn't care; she was leaving them behind anyway.

On the drive home, the Neymores spoke about Rachel, hoping Thalía and their daughter would become fast friends. They mentioned Rachel spoke some Spanish too, though she could use some practice. Thalía understood why they had chosen her and felt a surge of gratitude and excitement at the thought of leaving the group home and living with a real family.

Thalía and Rachel immediately hit it off. They bonded over shared experiences, supported each other, and quickly became the sisters they had never had. Thalía told Rachel about her cousin Marco and how determined she was to find her way back to her country to be with him. Rachel, who was tech-savvy and skilled at research, tried to help, but despite their efforts, they couldn't uncover any trace of Marco.

Life with the Neymores was a stark contrast to the group home. They had a beautiful house, and Thalía finally had her own bedroom.

She often expressed her gratitude to the couple for taking her in and caring for her.

One afternoon, Thalía and Rachel were having a girls' day, doing each other's makeup, styling their hair, and sharing laughs. Rachel commented on how beautiful Thalía was and admitted she wished she could look like her. Thalía smiled and reassured her, "You're beautiful too, Rachel. Don't ever think otherwise."

Trying to make herself less intimidatingly pretty, Thalía mentioned her heterochromia. Rachel asked, "What's that?" Thalía explained, "It's when someone has two different colored eyes. I wear a contact to hide it. My cousin Marco has it too, it's kind of our thing."

"Can you show me?" Rachel asked curiously.

Thalía laughed. "Sure, but don't be grossed out when I take it out."

Rachel replied immediately, "I could never be disgusted with you."

Thalía carefully removed her contact. Rachel's eyes widened. "Wow, that's so cool! Since you have brown and gray eyes, why don't you switch it up and wear a gray contact too? I think it would look amazing!"

Not expecting that type of reaction from Rachel, "Why not?" Thalía said. She reached into her bag, pulled out a gray contact, and placed it in her brown eye. Rachel gasped. "Wow! Now you're even more stunning!"

Thalía looked in the mirror, seeing herself with makeup, lipstick, and two gray eyes. "I think I'll keep this look for a while, a kind of fresh start," she said.

Rachel nodded. "It fits you perfectly."

Thalía grinned. "I wonder if Marco would look this good with makeup and gray eyes too," she joked. They both laughed and lay back on the bed, savoring the simple joy of the moment.

Even as she enjoyed her new life, Thalía often dreamed of finding Marco and bringing him to live with the Neymores, imagining a future where they were finally safe together.

Poor Little Poor Girl

CHAPTER 36

A Dangerous Realization

The next morning, Thalía and Rachel came down for breakfast. Rachel's parents were already at the table. As Thalía approached, Rachel excitedly pointed out her new gray contact lens, explaining how they had decided together to try a fresh look. Both parents smiled warmly at the girls. Mrs. Neymore said, "I'm so glad you two are getting along so well."

Thalía noticed Mr. Neymore giving her a peculiar look out of the corner of his eye. She assumed it was because of her different eye color, and remotely drastic change in appearance.

Thalía had now been living with the Neymore's for about nine enjoyable months, She had begun to truly feel at home with the Neymore's, finding comfort in their kindness, especially in the close bond she had formed with Rachel. Life seemed to settle into a routine.

She enjoyed her new surroundings and appreciated the Neymores' efforts to help her case move along. Mr. Neymore even called in a few favors from friends in the federal government to help expedite her return home. After all, her 18th birthday was approaching, and the process would become more complicated once she was no longer a minor.

The time had come for Rachel to leave for her two-week long summer camp in the mountains. She and her mother drove out for registration and orientation, knowing she would officially start camp in just two days.

Since the trip had been planned long before Thalía arrived, there was no way to include her. On top of that, Thalía had a scheduled appointment with her social worker that she needed to attend.

As Rachel prepared to leave, Thalía watched her give Mr. Neymore a long, loving hug and a tender kiss goodbye. Seeing the bond between father and daughter stirred a deep longing in Thalía, she wished she had a father who cared for her as much as she cared for him, someone who could give her that same unconditional love.

Mrs. Neymore and Rachel drove off, leaving Mr. Neymore and Thalía standing at the doorway, waving farewell. Thalía knew it would be at least a few hours before they returned, leaving just her and the mister alone in the house. Based on her past experiences, she felt uneasy, though she reassured herself that Mr. Neymore could never be like the others who had betrayed her trust before.

As soon as they were out of sight, Mr. Neymore instructed Thalía to go wash up so she would be ready for her appointment in town. She headed upstairs, got in the shower, began washing her hair, lost in her thoughts. Suddenly, a brief cool draft brushed against her skin, but she ignored it and went on, finishing the wash of her hair and body.

When she reached for the towel she had left on the rack, it was gone. Unsure what to do, she remained standing in the shower, soaked and shivering, with nothing to dry herself. Suddenly, a single knock came at the door. It was Mr. Neymore, asking if she needed a towel. Before she could respond, he had already opened the door and stepped inside.

Thalía froze as she stood naked, instinctively crossing her arms over her chest and stepping to shield herself behind the shower curtain, a rush of fear flooding her. He spoke casually, offering to help her dry off quickly so they could get on the road.

In that moment, a cold realization hit her, the brief draft she had felt earlier wasn't just a breeze. It had been him taking the towel, creating an excuse to enter the bathroom once he heard the water stop running. Her heart raced as she understood the danger of the situation, and she braced herself to handle it carefully.

Thalía's stomach churned with unease and fear as she realized what was unfolding. Every instinct screamed at her that this was wrong. Mr. Neymore, noticing her hesitation, spoke in a calm, coaxing tone, telling her not to say anything to anyone and insisting that this was just an "innocent" way to help her get ready faster.

As he moved the towel across her body, Thalía insisted, her voice trembling, that she could manage on her own. He waved it off casually, saying it was no big deal and that they were almost done. Thalía held her chin high and fought to hold back her tears, every muscle in her body tense with discomfort and fear.

Once again, a wave of betrayal washed over her, quickly turning into anger. If she couldn't trust Mr. Neymore, then who could she trust? Her mind raced with that terrifying thought.

He told her to go to her room, put oil on her skin, and that he had something special for her to wear. Heart pounding, Thalía didn't hesitate. She muttered, "ok, I'll go do that now". She hurried to her room, threw on jeans, a shirt, and sneakers, gathered a few belongings in a backpack, and then climbed out the window, running as fast as her legs could carry her.

She knew this was the only way to protect herself. She couldn't face reliving those nightmares again.

Although terrified and disappointed, she couldn't help but to think of Rachel, how much the girl adored her father, as well as how she knew Mrs. Neymore loved him. Thalía respected them both deeply and loved Rachel like a sister. She couldn't let their lives be torn apart by the betrayal she had just endured.

With that in mind, she ran. She never looked back. Staying wasn't an option, it never would have ended well.

This time, she would survive, and she would never let anyone control her again.

CHAPTER 37

The Lie

After a long silence, Mr. Neymore grew restless. Thalía had been gone too long. He strode to her bedroom door, knocked sharply, and called, "Are you almost ready?"

No answer.

Frowning, he pulled a thin tool from his pocket, slid it into the lock, and turned. The door creaked open. His eyes swept across the empty room—bed neatly made, window wide open. Thalía was gone.

For a moment, panic flickered in his eyes, but just as quickly it hardened into something colder, more deliberate. The muscles in his face pulled tight. He stood there, calculating.

By the time Mrs. Neymore and Rachel pulled into the driveway a while later, he was waiting on the porch, mask already in place.

"She's gone. Thalía's gone," he announced flatly, voice laced with feigned disappointment.

Rachel's heart lurched. "Gone? What do you mean gone?"

Mr. Neymore sighed, shaking his head as though burdened with regret. "I caught her stealing jewelry from your mother's vanity. When I confronted her, she panicked. Climbed out of the window and ran away before I could stop her."

Rachel's breath caught. "No, Thalía would never!"

But her father's lie was smooth, practiced. The seed was planted, and it would grow.

"I already called the police," he added, tone sharp, final. "It's out of our hands."

Mrs. Neymore gasped, clutching at her pearls. Rachel's chest ached with confusion, disbelief etched across her face. Yet Mr. Neymore didn't blink. The story was set.

Minutes later, flashing red and blue lights painted the front of the house. Inside, Rachel curled on the couch, hugging a pillow as tears streaked her cheeks. Mrs. Neymore paced the room, wringing her hands. Mr. Neymore stood tall near the door, his performance flawless: the disappointed father who had "done the right thing."

A knock rattled the door.

He opened it to find two uniformed officers. "Good afternoon, sir. We received a report about a theft?" Officer Hernandez asked.

"Yes, come in," Mr. Neymore replied, voice solemn. "A terrible situation."

The officers entered, scanning the tidy living room. Rachel sat up stiffly, hands trembling.

"Tell us what happened," Officer Hernandez prompted.

Mr. Neymore released a weary sigh, as if the memory weighed him down. "We had a young guest staying with us, that we brought from the Foster home. Her name is Thalía. A friend of my daughter's. This morning I found her going through my wife's jewelry box. She had pieces in her bag. When I confronted her, she bolted. Out the window."

Officer Lee scribbled notes. "You saw her take the jewelry?"

"I saw it in her hand," Mr. Neymore replied smoothly. Just enough hesitation to sound sincere. "She must have panicked."

Mrs. Neymore's voice cracked as she added, "I—I haven't even checked what else is missing yet."

Officer Hernandez nodded. "We'll need a list for the report."

Rachel's gut twisted. None of it made sense. Thalía stealing? Running away like a thief? This wasn't the girl who stayed up whispering secrets, who dreamed of finding her cousin, who had become her sister in everything but blood.

"Do you have a photo of her?" Officer Lee asked.

Rachel fumbled for her phone. "Yes." Her hand shook as she passed it over.

"Thank you," Officer Lee said gently. "We'll issue a Be On The Lookout (BOLO) for her. If she's nearby, we'll find her."

Rachel followed them onto the porch, unable to stay quiet. "Please… don't hurt her if you find her. Maybe there's more to the story."

Officer Lee gave her a puzzled look but softened. "We'll do our jobs, 'little missie'. Don't worry."

Rachel nodded weakly, though her heart churned with dread.

When the patrol car pulled away, silence returned. Mr. Neymore closed the door with a heavy thud. Turning back, he let out another rehearsed sigh.

"We did what we had to," he murmured.

Rachel stared at him, doubt gnawing deeper than ever. This was not Thalía! She wasn't sure if she believed him.

She wasn't sure if she believed *anything* anymore.

* * *

Hunted...

Thalía crouched low behind a thick row of hedges just off the main road, her damp clothes clinging to her skin. Every muscle in her body ached from running, but she didn't dare move. Her heart slammed against her ribs so violently she was certain the sound would give her away.

In the distance, she spotted them, two police cruisers rolling slowly down the street, headlights sweeping across lawns and driveways like searching eyes.

She pressed herself tighter to the earth, knees hugged to her chest, forehead resting against them. She willed herself smaller. Invisible.

They're looking for me, she realized, the thought striking harder than the cold ground beneath her.

Tears pricked her eyes, but she wiped them away with the back of her hand. Crying wouldn't save her. Thinking would. Surviving would.

The faint hum of police radios drifted through the air, fragments of words carried on the night breeze:

"...young Hispanic female..."

"...black hair, small build..."

"...considered a thief and a runaway..."

Her stomach twisted. *Thief? Runaway? Not victim? Not scared girl who escaped something terrible?*

Her throat closed, a heavy lump rising inside her. They didn't know the truth. Nobody did. And if she was caught, would anyone even listen? Mr. Neymore's lies were already painting her as the villain in a story she never chose to be part of.

The patrol cars slowed at an intersection. She knew she had seconds, maybe less. Biting her lip until she tasted blood, Thalía bolted.

Not toward town. Not toward the lights.

Into the woods.

The trees swallowed her whole, shadows clutching at her like living things. Branches ripped her sleeves, thorns carved scratches into her skin, roots clawed at her sneakers. Her lungs burned, her legs screamed, but she didn't stop.

She couldn't stop.

Because now Thalía understood the truth with a clarity that chilled her to the bone:

She wasn't just running away from a house.

She was running for her life.

And she would not let them catch her.

Poor Little Poor Girl

CHAPTER 38

Curiosity killed the cat

Rachel...

That night, the house felt wrong. Too quiet. Too heavy. The kind of silence that pressed down on Rachel's chest until it was hard to breathe.

Her father sat in his usual chair, a book open in his lap, but his eyes never touched the page. Instead, he stared straight ahead, expression calm, too calm. Her mother fussed with dishes in the kitchen, the soft clink of porcelain almost frantic, like she was trying to fill the silence.

Rachel sat on the couch, knees pulled to her chest. Her thoughts swirled so violently she thought she might be sick.

Thalía. Gone. Just like that.

She squeezed her pillow tighter. Her father's story replayed in her mind, word for word. The way he had spoken, so smooth, so certain. But she knew Thalía. She *knew* her. The girl who spent hours helping her cram for math tests. The girl who laughed so hard at corny jokes that her stomach hurt. The girl who once gave Rachel her last piece of candy, saying, "Best friends don't keep the good stuff to themselves."

That girl didn't steal. That girl didn't run away like a criminal.

Rachel glanced at her father. His jaw was tight, his knuckles pale against the armrest. Something about the way he held himself screamed restraint, as though his control might snap if she looked too closely.

Her chest tightened. *What if he… what if he did something?*

The thought made her stomach churn with guilt. This was her father. The man who taught her how to ride a bike, who carried her on his shoulders at the fair, who kissed her forehead goodnight. How could she even think it?

But the image of Thalía's open window haunted her. The curtains swaying in the breeze, no trace of a struggle, just absence. It felt too neat, too staged.

What if he made her leave? What if he's hiding something?

Rachel's throat burned as tears welled again. She wanted to believe him. She wanted to cling to the father she loved, the man who had always seemed unshakable, trustworthy. But every time she looked at him, that seed of doubt grew sharper, digging into her chest.

She finally conjured up the courage and asked softly, her voice trembling. "Dad?"

He turned his head, his face arranged into gentle patience. "Yes, sweetheart?"

She hesitated, her heart hammering. "Are you… are you sure that's what happened? With Thalía? Maybe she, maybe it was just a misunderstanding?"

His gaze hardened, just for a flicker, before smoothing over. "Rachel." His tone was firm, final. "I know what I saw. I don't like it any more than you do, but we can't change the truth."

Her lips parted, but no words came out. That flash in his eyes— cold, dangerous—left her frozen. It was gone in an instant, replaced by the father she knew. But Rachel had seen it.

And now, she couldn't unsee it.

She nodded faintly, pretending to accept his words, but inside, her chest ached with a growing certainty.

Her father wasn't telling the whole truth.

And if Thalía had really run away… it wasn't because she stole.

It was because of something else.

* * *

Rachel's silence stretched, heavy and brittle. Her chest ached with the weight of everything she couldn't say.

Her father leaned forward, resting his elbows on his knees, his voice low but edged with command. "Rachel. I need you to leave this alone."

She blinked at him, startled. "But"…

"NO!" The word cracked through the room like a whip. His eyes locked onto hers, unflinching. "You need to erase Thalía from your mind. She made her choice. And we… we need to move on with our lives. Do you understand me?"

Rachel's throat tightened. She wanted to scream that he was wrong, that she knew there was more to the story, but his stare froze her in place.

Across the room, her mother nodded numbly, dabbing her eyes with a tissue as if she needed her husband's words to steady her.

Mr. Neymore leaned back, his tone shifting to something almost casual, though the cruelty beneath it was unmistakable. "That's how those kids are from the foster home. You bring them in, think you can help, think you can fix them... but you can't. They're trouble. Always have been, always will be. We should have never let Thalía, or any of those kids, into this house in the first place."

The words struck Rachel like ice water. But she knew her father didn't mean those harsh words. She pulled her knees closer to her chest, her heart pounding.

Her father rose, placed a firm hand on her shoulder, and forced a thin smile. "It's done, Rachel. I'm sure she's far from here by now, and we'll never see her again."

Rachel didn't answer. She couldn't. Because deep down, every fiber of her being screamed that it wasn't over.

That Thalía was out there.

And that she would someday meet her again and get the whole truth.

CHAPTER 39

Fields of Fire

Marco...

As Marco stepped onto the manicured turf in his first semi-pro uniform, the weight of his journey pressed down on him, but he stood tall beneath it. His cleats bit into the grass, and his lungs filled with the heavy, electric air of purpose.

The stadium lights were nothing like the dust-paved fútbol fields of home.

It was finally happening.

He was nervous, of course. The older players were faster, harder, and played with the kind of confidence that came from years of battles on the field. But what Marco lacked in age, he made up for in raw, relentless fire. And that fire burned hotter with every reminder, Eleanor's quiet belief in him, Jared's steady mentorship, the hollow ache of Thalía's absence, and the promise he made to himself: *Never stop searching.*

He was the youngest on the team, but it didn't take long for the crowd to start whispering about him, the kid with the lion's drive. Marco darted across the field like a streak of intent, outpacing men much older than he, and weaving through defenders as if he belonged to the wind itself. With each game, he carved out a name of his own, one goal, one assist, one impossible play at a time.

Marco, ten games into the season, had played very well, exceeding expectations of everyone. Eleanor never missed a match. She watched from the bleachers with quiet pride, her calm warmth drawing people to her naturally. Parents trusted her, players respected her, and she carried herself like someone who had seen pain but learned to turn it into grace.

After a particularly fierce game—two goals, one assist, and a roaring crowd, Eleanor found herself seated beside a man in a tailored coat and dark sunglasses. Mr. Vargas. His son, Tomás, played midfield on the same team as Marco.

"Your boy is impressive," Mr. Vargas said, nodding toward Marco as the players left the field.

Eleanor smiled softly. "Oh, he's not mine. But he feels like mine sometimes. Marco's had a hard road... fútbol had been his saving grace."

Mr. Vargas tilted his head, intrigued. "He plays like someone fighting for more than a win."

Eleanor glanced at him, recognizing the rare opening to possibly gain compassion to someone who may be a VIP. "He is," she said, her voice steady but threaded with emotion. "He's lost people. Carries grief that would break most grown men, but he never lets it stop him. He plays for something bigger. To make a difference. To find his cousin. To build a life no one can take away."

Mr. Vargas studied her for a moment, then turned his gaze back to Marco, who was laughing with teammates, sweat and joy glinting under the lights.

"I heard that he's only fourteen?"

Eleanor nodded. "Big heart. Bigger vision."

Mr. Vargas was quiet for a long beat. Then he said, "He ever think about National Academies? Scouts? He's definitely good enough!"

Eleanor's smile dimmed, knowing reality and seizing another potential opportunity. "He dreams of it. But dreaming doesn't get you noticed. Someone has to open a door first."

* * *

Out of the Blue...

A few days later, Marco was called into Felipe's office after practice. His coach's grin gave everything away before he spoke.

"Marco, I don't know how this happened, or why, and I don't even care; but someone must have called in a favor for you. You've got a tryout with the National League!"

Marco froze, wide-eyed. "Me? Why?"

Eleanor, standing by the doorway, said softly, "Because you earned it. And because someone finally saw what I've always known."

The days leading up to the tryout blurred together. Eleanor handed him her old bracelet, a worn, silver band with a single charm shaped like a wing.

"It was mine when I was Thalía's age," she said, fastening it on his wrist. Thalía always admired this bracelet, and I was going to give it to her one day when the time was right. "I think she'd want you to wear it."

Marco hugged her tight. "Thank you... for believing in me."

Poor Little Poor Girl

CHAPTER 40

Tryouts

The air felt different in the capital.

Marco stepped off the bus into a world of towering buildings, glistening sports complexes, and young athletes with tailored duffel bags and polished cleats. Everything felt bigger, faster, and sharper here, but he walked with purpose.

Marco stepped through the gates of the professional training facility with his duffel bag slung over his shoulder, disbelief flickering behind his determined eyes. Only one-year ago, he'd been a street kid playing barefoot on dusty fields, now he was walking among professionals.

Reporters and spectators crowded near the entrance, whispering in awe about the fourteen-year-old phenom who'd climbed from local obscurity to national attention in less than a year. Cameras flashed, journalists called his name, but Marco kept his head down, heart steady. He wasn't here for fame, he was here to prove he belonged.

The opportunity of a lifetime was here. And he wasn't alone.

Tomás Vargas, his semi-pro teammate and son of the influential Mr. Vargas, had made it too.

Though Tomás had grown up with more than Marco ever had, they found themselves equals now. Both were talented. Both were hungry. And both had something to prove. For Tomás, it was escaping his father's shadow and earning respect on his own. For Marco, it was building something from nothing, and proving that he belonged.

At first, their interactions were simple. Quick nods in the locker room. Encouragement after drills. But after the first practice scrimmage, something clicked.

It happened mid-match. Marco intercepted a cross-field pass with the precision of a hawk and darted down the sideline. As defenders closed in, he noticed Tomás silently cutting across the box. Without thinking, Marco sent a slick, low pass between two defenders. Tomás connected cleanly and launched it into the top corner.

Goooaaal!!!

The entire camp turned toward the duo.

Later, during a tactical drill, it happened again. This time, Tomás lured a defender with a clever run and back-heeled a perfect ball into Marco's stride. Marco didn't even hesitate, he buried it into the net. Coaches glanced at each other with raised eyebrows.

By the third day, Marco and Tomás were a known duo.

"Those two..." one coach muttered. "They read each other like brothers."

Off the field, their bond grew. They shared meals, compared training routines, and swapped stories. Tomás confided in Marco about his struggles with being the son of a powerful man, the pressure to perform, and the loneliness that came with high expectations. Marco, in turn, opened up about Thalía, the saloon, and Eleanor's steady wisdom.

"I envy that," Tomás said one night as they lay in their dorm bunks. "Having people who believe in you without expecting you to be perfect."

Marco turned on his side. "And I envy you for having access to this world from the beginning. But I guess it's not really about where we started anymore. It's about what we do with the shot we've been given."

Tomás grinned. "Then let's make sure we both take it."

At the end-of-week showcase game, all eyes were on the players. Scouts, club officials, and national team reps packed the viewing boxes, their notepads ready.

Marco and Tomás delivered.

In the first half, they linked up beautifully: Tomás launched a long ball from midfield that Marco volleyed in with clinical precision. Later, Marco drew three defenders before slipping a cheeky pass through to Tomás, who scored with style. Their chemistry was electric—fast, intuitive, unselfish.

By the end of the game, the crowd had stopped keeping track of their individual plays. It was all about *them*, the duo.

After the match, as Marco toweled off on the bench, a familiar figure approached, Mr. Vargas. He looked between his son and Marco, eyes filled with pride and calculation.

"You two make quite a pair," he said. "Reminds me of some of the best duos I've seen in European academies. I've already had two calls asking about the boy from nowhere," he nodded toward Marco, "and now they're asking about you both."

Tomás beamed. Marco looked surprised.

"I'll say this once," Mr. Vargas added, "you both made an impression today. But this world is built on more than talent. It's about relationships. Image. Presence. Play smart, and doors will open."

Later that evening, Marco sat quietly on the rooftop balcony of the dorm, looking over the glowing skyline.

Tomás joined him, tossing a bottle of water into his hands. "To the next level?"

Marco nodded. "To the next level."

They clinked bottles, then looked out over the city.

Down below, deals were being made, futures were being drawn, and people in very high places were starting to whisper the names of *two* young boys with fire in their veins.

And somewhere deep in Marco's heart, he felt this was just the beginning.

The pro team's Administration and Owners requested a private sit-down with Marco and Eleanor after the showcase game.

"You've got something special, kid," one of the Administrators began, his tone serious but kind. "But we need to talk."

Marco's stomach tightened. The way they exchanged glances made him fear the worst, that his age had cost him the opportunity of a lifetime. "We're not here to waste anyone's time," another Administrator said, folding his hands on the table.

For a split second, Marco's heart sank. But then the man's expression softened.

"Bottom line, son, we're impressed. You've shown maturity, discipline, and raw talent beyond your years. Frankly, you dominated these tryouts. We just needed to make sure your guardian was on board."

Eleanor nodded her head up and down, as to say "yes", her eyes bright with pride.

The head Administrator leaned forward with a grin. "Then it's settled. Congratulations, young man, welcome to the pros. You're one of the youngest player ever to make it in!"

For a moment, Marco couldn't breathe. Then, slowly, the smile broke through. He'd done it.

At the tryouts, Marco played like a storm unleashed. Fierce. Fluid. Fearless. He didn't chase the ball, he commanded it. When the final whistle blew, he had received that beautiful gold business card with his name on it, saying that he has been accepted into the Professional Fútbol League.

Later that evening, Marco sat on the bottom bleacher in the stands, the card turning slowly between his fingers. The air smelled of light rain and grass. Eleanor sat beside him, silent for a moment before speaking.

"I still miss her," he said quietly.

"I know," she replied. "But she's in every step you take. Every door that opens for you, it opens for her too."

Marco nodded, his gaze fixed on the horizon. He didn't have all the answers, but he had direction. A path.

And maybe, just maybe, that path would lead him closer to peace, to purpose, and one day, to Thalía.

CHAPTER 41

It's Official

The following day, official player team assignments were to be posted. Although Marco felt confident after the meeting, he was still concerned for his friend Tomás Vargas. The campus was buzzing. Coaches walked with purpose, phones glued to their ears. Scouts from clubs all over whispered behind closed doors. Every player waited for one thing: the list, those who would receive official invitations to train abroad or join elite teams.

Marco tried to keep his head down, but the air around him crackled with expectation.

When the list finally went up, a crowd gathered around the bulletin board like bees to honey. Marco and Tomás made their way through the crowd, side by side.

There it was, now Official…

o **Marco Salazar – Barcelona Spain**

o **Tomás Vargas – Real Madrid**

They stood in silence for a moment, letting it sink in.

"Different cities," Tomás said with a faint smile. "But same country."

Marco laughed softly, though his chest felt tight. "We'll still see each other—friendlies, tournaments, cups."

Tomás held out his fist. "Next time we're on the field, we're rivals."

Marco bumped it. "But always teammates in here."

They both tapped their chests, grinning through the bittersweet goodbye.

* * *

Weeks Later – Spain...

Marco stepped into the Barcelona field like he was walking into another world. The air buzzed with precision. The buildings gleamed. Every player around him looked like they had been born into this life—scouted, polished, prepared.

He was the outsider.

And it showed.

In his first week, he missed a crucial run during a training match and got barked at, in three different languages. He tripped in front of one of the senior coaches. In the locker room, conversations died when he walked in.

It wasn't just failure that stung, it was loneliness.

Back in his dorm, Marco sat on his bed staring at his phone. Messages from home poured in:

Eleanor: "You're where you belong. Greatness comes with a little fire."

Camilla: "We miss you. Eat well. Be strong."

Jared: "Don't forget who you are. Saloon still standing. Work harder than everyone."

Then came the one that made him smile:

Tomás: "Rough start here too. Coach said I play like a 'flashy tourist.' Don't sweat it. We've got this."

It was enough to make Marco breathe again.

* * *

Two Months Later...

The tide began to turn.

Marco stayed after every practice, running sprints in the fading light, sharpening his first touch, studying film until his eyes blurred. Slowly, things shifted. Respect came, first from the coaches, then from the players. He started earning more minutes. More trust.

His passes split defenses. His goals drew gasps. His name began to carry weight.

During an international friendly in France, Barcelona faced Atlético Madrid.

Marco vs. Tomás.

Before kickoff, they met on the sideline, no cameras, no crowd, just two boys who had once chased dreams on a dusty field.

"Don't go easy on me," Marco smirked.

Tomás grinned. "Wouldn't dream of it."

The match was electric. In the 67th minute, Marco intercepted a lazy back pass, slipped past two defenders, and buried the ball into the bottom corner. Minutes later, Tomás answered with a blistering run and a curling strike that kissed the crossbar before finding the net.

Final score: **2–2.**

But both walked off as the stars of the match.

That night, Marco sat alone on his hotel balcony, the Paris skyline glowing in the distance. He pulled out his phone and opened a photo; him and Thalía as kids, laughing, kicking a worn soccer ball down a dirt road.

He smiled, a quiet ache in his chest.

Then he opened his notebook. On the first page, written months ago, were three goals:

1. Play professionally.

2. Send money home.

3. Find Thalía.

Two were now within reach.

The third still burned the brightest.

CHAPTER 42

Echoes of Her Name

It was raining the evening Marco got the call.

He stood in the hallway of Barcelona's stadium, towel slung over his shoulder, hair still damp from training. His phone buzzed in the locker, **unknown number.** Normally, he'd let it ring out, but something in his gut told him to answer.

"Hola?" he said cautiously.

"Marco Salazar?" came a low, accented voice. "This is Detective Raul Virella. I'm with the Missing Persons Unit in northern Argentina. You don't know me, but I believe I may have information about a person of interest to you."

Marco froze.

The hallway seemed to fade around him. His breath caught in his chest.

"Thalía?" he whispered.

A brief silence. Then the detective exhaled. "We don't know for certain. But we've had several sightings matching her description near a remote border town close to Bolivia. She's been using another name. Nothing confirmed, but enough for you to know."

Four years. Four long, silent years.

"Why now?" Marco managed.

"The girl's kept her distance. Locals say she's quiet, afraid of officials. But last week, someone reported she was drawing names in a notebook. One of the names was yours."

The detective paused. *"Marco, my special soccer player."*

Marco's knees buckled. He slid down against the locker, gripping the phone like it might vanish.

"Thank you," he said, voice breaking.

"We're not done yet," Virella replied. "But I'll keep you updated."

When the call ended, Marco sat in stunned silence, the rain outside echoing through the hallway. Then he stood and walked straight to the training office.

* * *

That same day, Coach Santino pulled him aside after practice.

"You have a visitor," the coach said, handing him a crisp envelope.

Inside was a contract, a professional offer from Barcelona. Promotion to the practice squad, with a starter's salary.

"The club believes in you," Santino said simply.

Marco stared at the paper, the words blurring. His body was in Spain, but his mind was thousands of miles away, in the jungles of Argentina, in the sound of the detective's voice, in the ghost of Thalía's laughter.

"You don't have to decide now," Santino added softly. "Take the weekend. Think it through."

* * *

That night, Marco called home. The connection crackled, but the voices were clear.

Jared leaned forward, eyes wide. "You heard from Thalía?"

Marco nodded. "A possible lead. Nothing solid. But... it's something. I'm going after it."

Eleanor's face filled the screen. "You're getting close, Marco. I can feel it. But remember, this contract, this opportunity... it's not just for you. It's for her too."

Camilla wiped her eyes. "You find her. And when you do, bring her home."

* * *

A Choice Made...

Marco signed the contract.

With his first paycheck, he sent money home, enough to fix the saloon roof, buy new books for the makeshift school, a new stove for Camilla, and a polished countertop for Jared's bar. For Eleanor, he bought a plane ticket. "For when you come visit," he wrote in the note.

Then, he called Detective Virella back.

"I want to go," Marco said. "If there's even a chance she's there, I need to see for myself."

Barcelona granted him a short leave of absence. Coach Santino clasped his shoulder.

"Some things are bigger than fútbol," he said. "Go find her. Then come back stronger."

Before leaving, Marco texted Tomás:

Marco:

"Got a pro contract. And maybe a lead on Thalía. It's happening."

Tomás:

"You're living two dreams at once, man. Go finish the one that matters most."

* * *

As the plane descended over the misty hills of northern Argentina, Marco stared out the window, heart pounding.

In his pocket—his first professional contract.

In his chest—a promise that refused to die.

He wasn't chasing fame or glory anymore.

He was chasing family.

He was chasing the truth.

He was chasing Thalía.

CHAPTER 43

Is it her?

The air in northern Argentina was thick with heat and dust.
Marco stepped off the small, rattling bus with a single bag slung over his shoulder. The morning sun was already fierce, shimmering off the tin rooftops of the border town of Villaflor. Street vendors were setting up their stalls, their voices calling over one another in rhythmic Spanish. Dogs wandered between legs, noses to the ground, and eyes of suspicion followed every stranger who passed through.

Waiting near the cracked concrete steps of the terminal was Detective Raul Virella, a tall, broad man whose silver-streaked hair hinted at years of quiet endurance. His handshake was firm, his expression unreadable.

"She goes by the name *Ana Lucia*," Virella said as they climbed into an old, dust-covered Land Cruiser. "Lives on the outskirts, works in a small canteen. Keeps to herself, doesn't trust easily. But…"he paused, glancing toward Marco, "she carved a names into the dirt wall of her room, yours. That's why I called."

Marco stared out the window as they drove. The streets blurred into dry fields and low adobe houses, his chest tightening with every mile.

He tried to imagine her—Thalía, as she might look now. Older, but still the same glimmer in her eyes. Would she recognize him? Would she even want to?

A thousand words rushed through his head: I never stopped looking for you.

I'm sorry I couldn't protect you.

But all he really wanted was to see her alive, to know that somehow, she had made it.

By the time they reached the canteen, the heat was sweltering. A corrugated metal roof sagged over a faded yellow building. Chickens scratched the dust outside, and a tiny radio played soft music from within.

Inside, the air was thick with the smell of oil and grilled corn. Dim light slanted through small windows, cutting through the haze.

And then he saw her.

A young woman, slender, her hair tied loosely back, a faded blue scarf hanging at her neck. She was pouring water into a glass, her movements careful, deliberate. Her head tilted slightly as she served a man seated at the far table.

Marco's heart seized. His breath caught in his throat.

"**Thalía...**" he whispered, stepping forward.

The girl looked up.

For a brief, fragile moment, the world went still. Her eyes met his, dark and uncertain, and for that single heartbeat, hope flared.

But then reality broke it apart.

Although she resembled Thalía, her face was different. Softer. Rounder. And her eyes, no heterochromia, both the same deep brown.

Not Thalía!

The girl frowned, confused. "¿Perdón, señor?"

Detective Virella placed a hand on Marco's shoulder. His voice was quiet, almost regretful. "Her name is really, Ana. My Argentinian contact arrived just minutes before us and questioned her. She told him that she didn't know you, "Marco Salazar, the famous fútbol player". She *was* indeed trafficked, yes, but from Bolivia. The name she wrote, 'Marco', was her brother's. He died years ago."

Marco said nothing.

He stepped outside, the sunlight blinding him. He sank onto the stone steps, resting his elbows on his knees and his head in his hands. The heat pressed down on him like the weight of failure itself.

He had crossed borders. Followed whispers. Hoped against reason.

But once again, it wasn't her.

Not Thalía. Not this time.

Only another wrong girl.

* * *

A few minutes later as the heat softened and the sound of distant traffic faded, Ana stepped quietly outside. She hesitated for a moment, then approached until she stood just a few feet from Marco, who sat slumped on the stone steps, staring at the dust beneath his boots.

"I'm sorry," she said softly. "You looked like someone I once knew too."

Marco nodded, his voice low. "You don't have to apologize."

He exhaled slowly, eyes fixed on the horizon. "I could have easily asked the detective if you had heterochromia, different-colored eyes. That would've told me right away you weren't her. But... for some reason, I didn't want to know. I wanted to see for myself. To look into your eyes and hope, just for a moment, that they'd be hers."

Ana's gaze softened. She knelt beside him, then handed him a small, cracked cup of water.

"Wherever she is," Ana said quietly, "she's alive. She's thinking about you. People who love like that... they leave marks. Maybe not in dirt. But in people."

Marco took the cup gently, his fingers brushing hers. "Gracias," he whispered.

Ana offered a faint smile before retreating inside, leaving him with the sound of chickens and the slow hum of the dying afternoon.

That night, Marco checked into a hotel near the edge of town. The fan above his bed creaked in lazy circles, stirring the heavy air. He lay on his back, staring at the flickering shadows on the ceiling, his mind replaying every moment of the day.

He reached for his phone to message Eleanor.

Marco:

It wasn't her.

Eleanor:

I'm sorry, my boy. That doesn't mean she's gone. Just that this wasn't the road.

Marco:

I'm tired. But I'm not done.

Eleanor:

Then rest. Come home. We regroup.

* * *

Back in Town and Ready for fútbol...

When Marco returned to Barcelona, there was something different about him. The boy who left searching for a ghost had come back with fire in his veins.

He didn't speak much. But when he stepped onto the training field, it showed.

Every touch of the ball was sharper, every sprint harder, every pass deliberate. The coaches noticed. His teammates felt it.

He had tasted disappointment, and it didn't weaken him.

It **refined** him.

Each strike, each play, each moment of focus carried the weight of something larger than ambition.

He wasn't just chasing a dream anymore.

He was honoring a promise—to the girl he couldn't find, but could never forget.

CHAPTER 44

The Promise Under the Lights

The roar of the stadium was deafening.

Marco was substituted into the game, due to an injury of one of the starters. He stood at the center of the field, sweat trickling down his back, cleats planted firmly in the pristine grass of Camp Nou. The moment he had dreamed of for years had finally arrived, a debut appearance for the senior squad of FC Barcelona.

The scoreboard blazed: Barcelona 2 – Sevilla 1.

And Marco Salazar, the kid from the saloon, had scored the winning goal.

The crowd chanted his name in unison, the rhythm echoing through his chest like a heartbeat:

"Maar-co! Maar-co! Maar-co!"

When the final whistle blew, he didn't raise his arms or leap in celebration. He simply kissed the bracelet around his wrist, Eleanor's gift, Thalía's memory, his anchor.

* * *

Later That Week – The Press Conference...

Marco sat before a wall of flashing cameras, a dozen microphones angled toward him. Reporters shouted over one another:

"Marco, how does it feel to score in your debut?"

"Do you see yourself on the World Cup squad?"

"Who was the goal dedicated to?"

He leaned forward, calm but steady.

"I want to take a moment," he said, "not just to talk about fútbol, but something that's near and dear to me!"

The room hushed.

"My cousin, Thalía Salazar, disappeared years ago. I've never stopped looking for her. I made a promise as a boy, and now that I finally have a voice, I intend to use it."

Silence spread like a wave.

"I'm asking anyone, anywhere, who has seen or heard anything about missing girls—especially in Central and South America, to come forward. My team has set up a private line and website. Every lead will be investigated."

By the time the conference ended, the headlines were already flashing across screens around the world:

BARÇA STAR MARCO SALAZAR LAUNCHES PERSONAL CAMPAIGN TO FIND MISSING COUSIN.

* * *

Behind the Scenes – New Connections...

In the weeks that followed, doors that had long been sealed began to open.

A retired Spanish diplomat who had admired Marco's play offered to connect him with humanitarian organizations. A Columbian senator, once close to Marco's teammate Tomás Vargas' father—granted access to sealed case files and national archives.

Even a journalist from Brazil reached out, proposing a feature story on Marco's mission and Thalía's disappearance.

Marco didn't chase fame. He chased leads.

When he wasn't training or playing, he was working, coordinating with lawyers, investigators, and private agents. He built a small, dedicated task force focused on finding Thalía and exposing the broader network that had stolen so many others like her.

He funded it all himself.

No press releases. No cameras.

Just quiet, relentless purpose.

* * *

The Photograph...

After a grueling match against Atlético, Marco returned to his apartment, his body aching but his mind alert. On the counter sat a plain envelope labeled **CONFIDENTIAL.**

Inside was a single photograph—grainy, printed from surveillance footage.

A young woman, late teens or early twenties, was stepping out of a small pharmacy in a Colombian border town. Thin. Pale. Wearing a red scarf around her neck.

On the back, a handwritten note read:

'*Possible match. Went by the name 'Thalía.'*

Marco sat down, gripping the photo in both hands. His breath caught in his chest.

Realizing because of his newfound status, his cause is gaining traction.

He didn't cry. Not yet.

Instead, he reached for the worn notebook he'd carried since his academy days and wrote:

"She's still out there.

I will find her."

* * *

The Fabulous Turf...

A week later, as the Anthem played and cameras panned across the lineup, Marco stood tall on the field once more. The cheers of eighty thousand fans washed over him, but his gaze was distant, searching the sea of faces in the crowd.

Somewhere out there, maybe watching from a dusty café or a flickering bootleg stream, was a girl he hadn't seen in years. A girl who once laughed beside him under a Honduran sunset and told him, *"We're gonna do big things, Marco."*

He whispered into the roar, almost to himself:

"I'm coming for you, Thalía."

On the field, Marco found his sense of safety and grace—a place where he could breathe, release his frustration, play hard, and set his troubles aside, even if only for a little while. After every game, he felt renewed. Out on the green, he felt stronger, protected. He even had a name for it: "The Fabulous Turf", because of how he felt while playing on it.

And as the whistle blew, Marco sprinted forward,

Not just chasing a ball.

But chasing a promise that still burned under the lights.

Poor Little Poor Girl

CHAPTER 45

Seeking Employment

Thalía...

After running away from the Neymores' house, Thalía had nowhere left to go. She spent a full day hiding on the streets, hungry, tired, and scared. Every sound made her flinch, every shadow felt like danger. But even through her fear, one thing was certain: she couldn't go back to the group home.

With no other options, she returned to the only place she thought might show her kindness, Cynthia's Diner.

When Cynthia spotted her standing hesitantly in the doorway, clothes rumpled and eyes weary, her face softened. "You again," she said, walking around the counter.

Thalía lowered her gaze. "I just... I need something to eat. Maybe a job, if you're still hiring."

Cynthia sighed deeply, resting her hands on her hips. "Sweetheart, I'll give you a meal and something to drink, no problem there. But I can't let you stay out here like this. You either go back to that group home, or I'll have no choice but to call the police again. I mean it this time."

Thalía's face fell, but Cynthia continued, her voice gentler now. "These streets aren't kind to a pretty young girl like you. My heart and my conscience won't let me just leave you out there."

For a moment, Cynthia's eyes drifted toward the diner window, her voice trembling ever so slightly. "I wish someone had done that for my daughter. Haven't heard from her in a long while. Folks say they still see her around sometimes, so at least I know she's alive. But what I wouldn't give to have her back in my life." She shook her head, collecting herself. "I messed up once, Thalía. I won't be part of messing up another young girl's life."

Cynthia led Thalía to a booth near the back and brought her a hot plate of food, eggs, toast, and a steaming cup of coffee. Then she handed her a small plastic bag with basic toiletries inside: a toothbrush and toothpaste, a small bar of soap, a comb.

Digging into the cash register, Cynthia pulled out a twenty-dollar bill and slid it across the table. "Here. Don't spend it all in one place, hun," she said with a faint smile. "When you're done eating, go freshen up in my private restroom in the back. I'll take a look at those scrapes afterward."

Cynthia moved off to tend to other customers, leaving Thalía to eat in peace. The first few bites hit her like warmth after a long winter, each mouthful a reminder of what it felt like to be cared for.

But then, out of the corner of her eye, she saw a police cruiser pull up outside. Panic flared in her chest.

She didn't know that Officer Rob, was one of Cynthia's regulars. All she could think of was the last time the police had come for her, and the words Mr. Neymore had twisted into lies.

So, when Cynthia disappeared into the kitchen to grab another order, Thalía slipped out the door, her half-eaten plate still warm on the table.

Moments later, Cynthia returned to find the booth empty. Happy that she at least took the twenty on the table, then her attention spanned to the door as Officer Rob stepped inside. Realizing what had happened, she sighed a quiet, weary sound, and went back to serving her customers, worry creasing her brow.

Thalía, meanwhile, wandered through the streets again, unsure where to turn. A few blocks down, she noticed a "Now Hiring" sign taped to the window of the bus stop booth. Hope stirred.

She made her way to the train station on foot, used the toiletries Cynthia had given her to clean up in the restroom, and caught a train heading across town toward the south side of Miami.

When she stepped off, the sun was sinking low, bathing the streets in orange. She wasn't exactly sure where the restaurant was, so with the paper she ripped from the bus stop booth in hand she began walking, scanning the buildings for any sign of it.

That's when a girl about her age approached—tall, blonde, and dressed in bright, flashy clothes. She wore an easy smile that didn't quite hide the curiosity in her eyes.

"You okay, sweetie? You lost?" she asked.

Thalía shook her head shyly. "I'm fine, thank you. I'm just looking for the Billings Tree Restaurant. I heard they're hiring, and I was hoping to get a job there. Do you know where it is?"

The girl tilted her head. "Sure, it's about two blocks down on your right." Then, with a laugh that carried more bitterness than humor, she added, "Can't imagine why you'd want to work there. That place is a shit-bag, and the customers? Even worse."

Thalía forced a small smile. "I don't have many choices right now."

The girl's expression softened. "Yeah... I get that."

Then, without another word, she crossed the street and leaned into the window of a car that had just pulled up, chatting easily with the driver as if they were old friends.

Thalía hesitated for a moment, unsure what to make of it, then continued down the street toward the restaurant, hopeful, but already feeling the weight of another long day pressing down on her.

* * *

The Interview...

Thalía arrived at the restaurant and stepped inside, taking in the dim lighting and the clatter of plates and voices. The owner, a burly man with a sharp gaze, greeted her curtly. "Take a seat over there," he said, pointing to an empty table in the corner. "I'll be right over to interview you."

Thalía sank into the chair, her stomach knotting with nervous anticipation. Around her, the customers were loud, boisterous, and rude, their laughter sharp and brash. It wasn't the kind of place she'd have imagined working, but she had nowhere else to turn. She clenched her fists under the table and reminded herself, *I have to try.*

Thirty minutes passed. Thalía watched as the owner conducted interviews with other people, his attention focused on each candidate in turn. Finally, he stood, hugged one of the women, and said with a smile, "Congratulations, you're the one." The girl beamed, leaving Thalía with a hollow knot in her chest.

The owner then approached her table. "No need for any more interviews," he said cheerfully. "I've found my girl."

Thalía's disappointment flared into anger. "Please," she said, her voice shaking slightly. "Just give me a chance. I'm capable of doing this job."

The owner regarded her with a kind but firm smile. "No offense, little girl, but this is a rough environment. It'll tear a pretty young thing like you apart. You'd be safer elsewhere."

Her shoulders slumped, and she rose, stepping out into the humid Miami air. Frustration and a sense of helplessness weighed on her chest. As she reached the stop sign across the street, she saw the girl from earlier leaning casually against the curb.

"So," the girl said, her tone dripping with sarcasm, "how'd your interview go?"

Thalía shook her head. "I didn't get the job."

The girl laughed, a throaty, unrestrained sound. "Good. That's probably for the best. Restaurant jobs suck, I should know." She extended her hand. "Hey, I'm Amy. And look, I've been exactly where you are. I saw it in your face the moment I walked over: fear, despair, uncertainty. Right?"

Thalía hesitated, then nodded reluctantly. "Yes. That's... exactly right."

Amy's expression softened, the teasing tone replaced by warmth. "Look at you," she said, her eyes scanning Thalía's face. "You're a pretty girl. But these streets will chew you up if you let them. Tell me, do you have a place to stay tonight?"

"No," Thalía admitted quietly.

Amy's lips curled into a half-smile. "I don't usually do this, but... you can crash at my place for a bit, until you can get on your feet."

Thalía blinked in surprise. "Are you sure? You don't even know me."

"I don't have to," Amy replied confidently. "To know you, I just need to see the fight in your eyes. And trust me, I see it. I've been where you are. I know exactly how it feels." She grabbed Thalía's hand, pulling her along. "These streets are full of struggle, but a girl's gotta do what she's gotta do to survive. And you? You're a survivor. I can feel it in you."

They walked together through the evening streets, the city's noise fading into the background as Amy led Thalía to her apartment. When they arrived, Thalía's jaw dropped. The space was bright, spacious, and immaculate, furnished with taste, decorated with care. Shiny appliances gleamed in the kitchen, and the wardrobe held clothes that looked far beyond her reach.

As she stepped inside, memories of Amy approaching that stranger at the street corner came back to her. Slowly, pieces began to click together. The way Amy carried herself, the apartment, the lifestyle, it all made sense now.

Thalía swallowed hard, a mix of awe and apprehension settling in her chest. She wasn't sure what the future held, but at least, for now, she had a place to rest and someone who seemed to care.

CHAPTER 46

The Knock at the Door

A week had passed, and Thalía still hadn't found a job. Each morning, she woke before Amy, quietly scrolling through online listings or walking to nearby stores to ask if anyone was hiring. Every evening, she came home empty-handed.

She hated the feeling, the quiet guilt that grew inside her each time Amy brushed it off.

"Girl, you're fine," Amy would say, waving her hand with that easy laugh. "I know you're looking. You'll find something soon. You're safe here, don't worry about it."

But Thalía *did* worry. She didn't want Amy to think she was taking advantage of her kindness. Amy had given her shelter, food, even laughter, things Thalía hadn't had in a long time. She wanted to help, to contribute, to feel like she belonged.

Then one afternoon, everything changed with a *hard, urgent knock* at the door.

Amy froze for a moment, then smoothed her hair and walked over to answer it.

The man who stepped in was tall, sharp-eyed, and carried an energy that made the air feel heavier. He looked Thalía up and down.

"Who's this?" he asked, his tone skeptical.

Amy forced a smile. "Oh, this? This is my cousin , she's just visiting from out of town."

The man smirked. "Yeah? She *better* be your cousin."

Amy giggled nervously, but there was no humor in it. "Jerry, don't start."

"Hey," he said, stepping closer, "you got that for me?"

Amy nodded quickly. "Of course, Daddy." She reached into her purse, pulled out a wad of cash, and handed it over.

From the couch, Thalía's stomach twisted. She pretended to focus on the TV, but her eyes flicked toward them, trying to make sense of what she was seeing.

Jerry noticed. His gaze snapped to her. "What the fuck you looking at, bitch?"

Thalía immediately looked away, her heart pounding.

"Jerry," Amy said sharply, stepping between them, "don't talk to her like that. She's got nothing to do with this."

Jerry's eyes narrowed. "What'd you say, bitch?"

Before Amy could respond, his hand flew across her face, the crack echoed through the small apartment.

Thalía shot to her feet, instinctively stepping toward Amy. Jerry turned on her, towering over her.

"What?" he barked. "You want some of this too?"

Thalía froze, every muscle in her body locked in fear.

"Jerry, stop!" Amy pleaded, her voice trembling. "She didn't do anything. It's my fault. Please. It won't happen again."

Jerry glared at both of them, his nostrils flaring. Then, with a grunt, he snatched the money from Amy's hand, muttered something under his breath, and stormed out, counting the bills as the door slammed behind him.

The silence that followed was suffocating.

Amy stood there for a moment, eyes glistening, one hand pressed to her cheek. Thalía slowly reached out, unsure if she should speak.

"Amy... why do you let him, "

"Don't," Amy cut her off softly. "You don't understand." She sat on the couch, staring at the floor. "Jerry's done things for me that no one else would've. Without him... I don't even know if I'd be alive. I owe him."

Thalía wanted to argue, to tell her that *no one* deserved that kind of treatment, but Amy's voice carried so much conviction that she didn't know how to respond.

Fifteen days passed. Thalía turned eighteen. Despite everything, her bond with Amy grew stronger. Amy was silly, unpredictable, and full of energy, always finding ways to make Thalía laugh when life felt too heavy.

Then, finally, Thalía found a job.

It wasn't glamorous, working in elder care, cleaning homes, shopping for groceries, caring for the sick and old. But it was *honest*. She was paid in cash, and that was enough.

A few months later, things were steady. Not perfect, just *steady*. Whenever Jerry came over, Thalía made herself scarce, leaving the apartment until he was gone. She didn't like the man, didn't trust him, but she knew better than to cause trouble.

Then, one week, everything shifted again.

At work, one of Thalía's coworkers suddenly quit. "I'm done," the woman said. "That crazy old man? The one who throws his shit on people? Not me. I'm out."

Thalía's boss sighed and turned to her. "Thalía, I'm reassigning you. You'll take over his care."

Thalía's stomach dropped. "But,"

"No 'buts.' It's part of the job, plus look on the bright-side, it's like a raise so you'll be making more money."

Her first day with the new client was worse than she could've imagined. The man was bitter and unpredictable. When she went to change his diaper, he grabbed a handful of feces and *threw it at her*. It splattered across her arm and chest.

He laughed, a cruel, childish laugh that echoed in her ears.

Thalía froze, biting down on every emotion clawing at her throat. Then she quietly cleaned and disinfected herself, cleaned *him*, and finished the shift in silence.

When she got home, she burst through the door, shaking with anger. "Amy, you won't believe what happened!" she cried, recounting every disgusting detail.

Amy's face twisted in disgust. "Girl, see? That's *exactly* why you need to quit that shitty job, literally! You can do better than that."

Thalía shook her head. "Right now, I don't have anything else. You know how hard it was to even get this one, especially without papers."

Amy sighed, pulling her into a quick, tight hug. "You're tougher than I thought, Thalía. Just... don't let the world break you, okay?"

Thalía nodded, resting her head against Amy's shoulder.

She wasn't sure if she could promise that, but she knew she'd try.

* * *

Persuasion...

Amy leaned against the counter, watching Thalía pace the small living room. "Girl," she said finally, her tone soft but deliberate, "you're too pretty to be wasting your time cleaning up after old folks. You could make real money."

Thalía frowned. "What do you mean?"

Amy tilted her head. "I used to work at the strip joint downtown, *La Rouge.* I still know a few of the girls there. They'd hook you up in a heartbeat. You could make more in one night than you do in a month scrubbing toilets."

Thalía hesitated, her eyes falling to the floor. "Amy... there's something I've been wanting to tell you. Things only very few people know."

Amy nodded, sensing the change in her tone. "Okay," she said quietly, "I'm listening."

Thalía sat down, her voice trembling as she began. "When I was little, my cousin and I... we watched our parents get gunned down by mercenaries. My father, " She swallowed hard. "He took the last bullet that was meant for me."

Amy's expression softened, her usual sarcasm replaced by concern.

"That's why my cousin and I have such a bond," Thalía continued. "It's unbreakable. He's the only family I have left, and I *have* to find him again someday."

Amy reached across the table, placing her hand gently over Thalía's.

Thalía took a shaky breath. "Growing up in Honduras was... hard. Poverty. Drugs. Death. No real medical care. And trafficking— everywhere. I think that's what happened to me. People always said I was pretty, and I think that's why they took me. Because of my looks." Her eyes welled up. "It's why I feel some type of way about compliments. They remind me of everything I lost."

Amy squeezed her hand. "Listen to me, Thalía. You can't go the rest of your life blaming yourself because you were born beautiful. There are sick people in this world, evil ones. But what happened to you wasn't your fault. You hear me?"

Thalía nodded slowly.

Amy continued, "You were a kid. You didn't choose poverty. You didn't choose what they did. But you *can* choose how you move forward. Stop looking back, baby. The past doesn't deserve you anymore."

Thalía wiped a tear from her cheek and smiled faintly. "You're right. I just... I don't know if I could do what you do. I've never danced before, and the thought of being naked in front of strangers? I'd die of embarrassment."

Amy burst out laughing. "Oh, please! I could teach you a few moves that'd make 'em throw their wallets on the stage." She flipped her hair dramatically and struck a pose. "I used to be a *bad bitch* on that pole! But this new hustle? Makes me even more money, and I don't even have to wear heels."

Thalía couldn't help but laugh. "You're crazy!"

"I know!" Amy said proudly.

Then, all of a sudden, Amy's eyes lit up with mischief. "Hold up, I got something for you." She darted into the kitchen and rummaged through the cabinet.

Thalía squinted. "What are you doing?"

Amy turned around, grinning devilishly, holding a jar of Nutella behind her back. "You'll see."

Before Thalía could react, Amy scooped out a handful and *flung* it across the room, splattering it across Thalía's arm.

Thalía froze, then burst out laughing. "Oh my God, you're insane!"

Amy doubled over, giggling uncontrollably. "Hey, if that old man can throw shit at you, I can too, but at least mine smells like chocolate!"

Thalía laughed so hard she could barely breathe. She grabbed the jar, scooped out some herself, and smeared it across Amy's cheek. "How do *you* like it now, huh?" she teased, mimicking the old man's raspy voice.

Within seconds, the apartment turned into a ridiculous, sticky mess; both of them laughing, ducking behind furniture, smearing Nutella on each other like two carefree kids who'd forgotten the world for a moment.

After endless months of struggle, she finally *felt alive.*

Then—BAM! BAM! BAM!

A hard knock shook the door. Both of them froze.

They knew that knock.

Amy's laughter vanished instantly. Her face drained of color.

Jerry.

Before either could move, the door crashed *open*, Jerry stormed in, his face twisted with rage.

"What the hell is going on in here?!" he barked, his eyes darting between the two girls, the smeared Nutella all over the floor, walls, tables, and overturned couch cushion.

Thalía's heart sank. The air felt cold again.

The laughter died.

The danger had returned.

CHAPTER 47

Survival of the Fittest

When Jerry burst through the door, the sound of splintering wood silenced the laughter in an instant. He stood in the doorway, eyes wide with fury, taking in the sight of Amy and Thalía smeared in Nutella and the mess around the apartment.

"What the hell is going on here?!" "Are ya'll covered in SHIT?!" he shouted.

Amy, trying to stay calm, forced a shaky laugh. "Nothing, baby. We're just having a little fun."

Jerry's expression darkened. "Fun? This is how you treat all the expensive shit I've been buying you? If all you're gonna do is fuck it up, then I'll do that for you."

Before either of them could respond, Jerry pulled out his pocketknife. With violent precision, he began slashing the couch cushions, yanking down the drapes, and throwing objects across the room. Glass shattered. Amy screamed. Thalía backed into the corner, frozen with fear.

Jerry turned sharply toward Amy. "And what is *she* still doing here? I've heard this ain't really your cousin, that she's been staying here in *my* damn apartment the whole time."

He stormed into the bedroom, rifling through drawers until he found Thalía's belongings. "You think you can hide shit from me?" he barked, slicing through her clothes. Then, glaring back at Amy, he hissed, "She better get the fuck out of my apartment. And I better *never* see her here again."

He moved closer to Amy, eyes burning. "You're lucky I don't want to mess up my product, or I'd slit this bitch's face." With that, he pressed the knife flat against Amy's shoulder and dragged the blade downward, barely deep enough to scratch her shin, cutting about three inches long. Amy cried out in pain.

"Next time, it's gonna be your face," he warned.

Thalía screamed, "Please stop! I'll go! You'll never see me again, I promise, just don't hurt her anymore!"

Jerry smirked. "You're lucky I'm feeling generous today. You got five minutes to get your shit and get out."

Thalía ran into the bedroom, heart pounding. Her clothes were torn and scattered, but she stuffed whatever she could grab into her bag. In her frantic rush, she accidentally scooped up some of Amy's things, including a small photograph of Amy and her mother.

When she emerged, Jerry was still yelling at Amy. Thalía hesitated only long enough to look back, eyes full of sorrow. She whispered, "Please be safe," and ran out into the cold night.

Minutes later, Jerry slammed the door behind him and left the apartment. Amy, trembling, dialed Thalía's number. "I'm sorry," she cried. "Where will you go? Do you have anyone to stay with?"

Thalía's voice was shaky but determined. "Don't worry about me. Worry about yourself. You need to get away from him before he kills you. I'll be fine. There's a diner owner I know, she'll help me figure something out."

Amy defended him even then. "He'd never seriously hurt me. He just gets mad sometimes. He was only trying to scare you and me."

The next morning, Amy called again, asking to meet and bring Thalía the rest of her belongings.

"Are you sure it's safe?" Thalía asked.

"Yes," Amy replied softly. "He's gone. I won't see him for another week."

Thalía said, "I'm staying at a small hotel—the diner owner I told you about signed for the room so I'd have a place until I can find somewhere permanent." She then texted her the address for where they could meet.

When Amy arrived, they embraced tightly, both apologizing through tears. Thalía glanced at her bandaged arm. Amy tried to brush it off. "It's just a scratch. He didn't want to do any real damage. It would mess up his 'business.'"

Amy sat on the edge of the bed and looked around the small room. "What are you going to do now? You've got no job, no home... what's next?"

Thalía shook her head. "I don't know. I can't go back to the group home, I've aged out. I just... I don't know."

Amy sighed. "Well, you have the hotel for now. You've got beauty on your side. You could do what I do from here. You'd make real money, fast."

Thalía's eyes widened. "No, Amy. You *know* what I've been through. You know why I can't do that."

Amy leaned forward, her tone growing serious. "Listen, Thalía. It's survival of the fittest out here. You've survived worse. You can survive this. It's raining and cold outside. You'll have no food, nowhere to go. I wish I could help you more, but you know who's in control."

Thalía was silent, staring at the floor.

Amy took her hand. "I'll help you through your first one. After that, you can decide if you want to keep doing it. Think about it, Thalía. Eight months of working these streets, and you could make enough money to go back home to find your cousin."

After a long silence filled with conflicting thoughts and tears, Thalía finally nodded. "Okay," she whispered. "I'll give serious thoughts about trying it."

CHAPTER 48

A Fragile First Step

Thalía's heart thudded in her chest. Tonight was the night, her first "date."

Amy had arranged it with one of her regular clients, assuring Thalía over and over that he was safe, respectful, and "one of the good ones."

"You'll be fine, baby," Amy said softly, brushing a strand of hair from Thalía's face. "He's been coming to me for years. Trust me, he's gentle."

Thalía managed a nervous smile. The reassurance helped, but only just. Deep down, a coil of fear still twisted in her stomach.

When the knock finally came at the door, her breath caught.

This was it.

She opened the door slowly. The man standing there smiled wide, eyes lighting up as he took her in.

"Wow," he said with a delighted laugh. "You are stunningly beautiful, just like Amy promised! And I love your eyes."

"Thank you," Thalía murmured, stepping aside to let him in.

He handed her the envelope of cash, then began to undress with casual ease. Thalía hesitated, her hands trembling as she slowly slipped out of her clothes, stopping at her underwear.

The man noticed her pause.

"Hey, everything okay?" he asked, brow creasing. "You're not... the police or something, right? This isn't a sting?"

Thalía shook her head quickly, wide-eyed.

He chuckled, relaxing. "Of course not. Amy wouldn't set me up like that."

Then, more gently, "She told me you're new. I'll be easy with you, I promise."

In just his boxers, he stepped closer, wrapping his arms around her. His body was warm, his scent faintly musky. He guided her toward the bed, laying her down softly and pressing his lips to hers.

Thalía froze.

Her mind flickered, flashes of dark rooms, strange hands, whispered threats, the sound of her own crying.

She pulled back, shaking her head. "I—I can't do this," she whispered, voice trembling. "I'm sorry."

She reached for the envelope on the nightstand, thrusting it toward him. "Please, take your money back. Just... please go."

He sighed, frustration flashing in his eyes. "Sweetie, come on. You're so beautiful. I'll be gentle, I promise."

But when she pushed him away again, firm this time, elbows braced against his chest, he stopped. He stared at her for a long moment, then exhaled heavily.

"You don't know how frustrating this is," he muttered. "But... fine. I'll respect your decision."

He gathered his clothes and headed for the door.

"Tell Amy she owes me big," he said before leaving.

* * *

The next day, Amy burst into Thalía's hotel room, visibly upset.

"Thalía, what happened last night? That guy wouldn't hurt a fly!" she said, pacing. "He's one of my best clients. You embarrassed me, girl. Now I've got to give him two free sessions just to smooth things over!"

Thalía's eyes filled with tears. "I'm sorry, Amy. I thought I could do it, I really did—but when he touched me... I just couldn't. It all came rushing back."

Amy threw her hands up. "You said you were ready! I thought you were over it, ready to move forward." Her voice cracked, half anger, half heartbreak. "I'm not trying to pressure you, baby, but if you can't do this... you might as well jump off a bridge, because no one's coming to save you!"

Thalía sobbed, covering her face. "I just need a little time," she pleaded. "Please. I'll try again soon. I promise."

Amy stood still for a moment, her anger softening. She sighed and sat beside Thalía on the bed, taking her hand.

"Look at me," she said gently. Thalía lifted her tear-streaked face.

"Listen, you only do what *you* can handle, okay? No one can make you do something you don't want to do. Stay true to yourself. Somehow, you'll make it through."

Her voice softened even more. "I really was trying to help you, Thalía. My way may not be the best way—but it's a way. I just wanted you to have a chance to survive. You hear me? You don't owe me anything. Just be true to yourself. No matter what, I'll always love you."

Thalía nodded through her tears. The two women embraced, their shoulders trembling as they cried together.

Then Amy's phone rang. The vibration buzzed against her leg, breaking the silence. She pulled it out, glanced at the caller ID, and her eyes widened.

On the screen, the name flashed:

'Cith'.

The nickname she only used for one person.

Her mother.

Amy says "excuse me, I have to take this call in private", and hurries off. Thalía thinks nothing of it, and says, OK, I will see you later. As Amy is walking away, Thalía hears her ask (rudely), "how did you get this number"?

* * *

Betrayal on the Block...

For days afterward Thalía replayed her conversation with Amy like a small prayer: Amy believed in her. Amy had offered a door. Thalía wanted to make Amy proud, wanted to prove she could do this on her own, that she could take a fragile step forward and stand on her own two feet. So that night she dressed in the slinkiest clothes she owned and went back out into the street alone.

The city's neon glowed against wet pavement. Men leaned on car hoods or idled at corners, eyes measuring every young woman who walked by. Thalía moved like she had practiced it a thousand times, though inwardly each step felt like stepping across glass. She tried to screen them from a distance, listening for the tone that felt safest. It was harder than she had imagined.

A woman on the sidewalk, blunt and tired-eyed, barked at her out of nowhere: "You're never gonna make any money if you keep shunning clients away." The practical cruelty in the woman's voice hit home. Thalía swallowed. She didn't want to disappoint Amy. She didn't want to be a burden. Decision hardened into necessity.

She believed the woman was right; She says to herself, "all I had to do is make a decision". A car passed by her twice, but on the third occasion, it slowed down significantly, and he finally invited her to join him. Initially, she had glimpsed what seemed like silhouettes of others in the backseat during the first two passes. Because the windows were darkly tinted she wasn't sure. However, this time, with the windows rolled down, she saw clearly that the backseat was empty.

The driver's approach was nice and respectful, she decided this was it, she's going to go with this guy and start making money. She told the guy she will go with him on the one condition that he must come to her hotel as she does not feel comfortable going to his house or hotel.

He says yes that's fine with me. So she got in the car and off they went back to her hotel room.

The guy seemed respectful, wasn't pushy, trying to rush her or anything. He placed the money on the nightstand, kept his hands gentle. Thalía convinced herself she could do it this time. She felt the old panic at the edges, but she told herself she could push through. When the moment came and she stood in her underwear, the world narrowed to two heartbeats. Then the dizziness of memory crashed in, images of dark rooms, hands that weren't gentle, orders barked in foreign voices. She trembled.

"I'm sorry," she said, voice a thin wire. "I can't. I just can't."

She handed back the envelope and reached for clothes.

From outside came the hard slam of a car door. The client rose and opened the door—and there, in the hallway, stood a second man, flanked by Jerry (Amy's Pimp).

Everything went cold.

Jerry didn't hesitate. He barged in, the door rattling off its hinges. Without preamble he smacked Thalía's face that sent her sprawling to the floor. Pain flared hot and immediate; the room spun. Jerry's voice filled the room, rough and triumphant. "You think you can work *my* block, bitch, and I don't find out?" He spat the words, each one a verdict. "I knew it was you the first time we drove round. We hid in the trunk. We set your ass up."

He paced as if the apartment were his stage, eyes hunting for Amy's name. "Where's Amy? Is she here?" Thalía, cradling her cheek and taste of blood in her mouth, shook her head and sobbed, "No, no, she's not here. I did this by myself."

Jerry laughed like it was proof enough. "If that bitch had anything to do with this, I'll beat her worse next time. Put her in the hospital." He dropped into a chair, lit a cigarette, and blew smoke like a command.

"Now you about to pay for trying to work on my block bitch," he said, flat and final. He nodded at the two men with him and says, "Handle y'all bizzness."

The two men attacked, smirking like predators. One of them says, "We're gonna have so much fun with you, I've been horny as hell for a week"! For a second shock froze Thalía, then something else took over, the instinct to survive. She rose and took up a fighting stance, desperate and furious. The goons laughed at the sight of her little frame squared off against them. One of them took a mocking step forward. Thalía remembered Eleanor's training—precise, spare moves meant to buy time and space. She caught the first man off guard, a sharp, clean strike that sent him stumbling backward. She twisted and aimed a kick at the second man's groin; he backed off, more annoyed than harmed.

For a few seconds the room became a flurry of motion: elbows, grunts, a sudden edge of hope. She landed blows, stole a breath, and tasted the small, but fierce joy of resistance. But two grown men coordinating together were a different kind of force. They recovered, closed the distance, and the balance shifted. Hands grabbed, pushed, and dragged her down. The last thing she registered with any clarity was Jerry's voice hollow and amused as he watched, cigarette ember glowing.

Afterwards there were no cinematic rescues, no last-minute saints. The men left as they had come—brutal, indifferent, and smelling faintly of smoke. Jerry flicked the cigarette ashes over her body and walked away with the same casual cruelty he wore like a badge.

Thalía lay on the floor for a long time, the room a scatter of overturned pillows. Her breathing came in jagged pulls. Shame and fury and the cold flattening weight of defeat rolled through her, but underneath them all, a small ember of something else smoldered: the part of her that had fought back.

The goons had assaulted her while Jerry stood by, encouraging them with cruel delight. She crawled to the bed, pulled a blanket around her, and pressed her face into it until the world blurred.

Outside, sirens might have wailed at some distant corner of the city, but not near enough. For now, there was only the ache and the decision ahead, how to take the next step, and whether she could still trust anyone to walk it with her.

CHAPTER 49

Recovery and Resilience

For the days following the attack, Thalía kept to herself, avoiding almost everyone, including Amy. The memory of Jerry's intrusion and what the men had done to her haunted every thought. Amy had confided that Jerry had bragged about it afterward, and the guilt weighed heavily on her. But Thalía, in her quiet strength, refused to let guilt define her.

Going to the police was never an option in her mind. She knew that being undocumented would only complicate things further. Worse, she feared what Jerry might do to Amy if law enforcement became involved. Instead, she took control in the only ways she could.

She called Amy and reassured her, softly but firmly, that it wasn't her fault. "I don't blame you," Thalía said. "And you shouldn't blame yourself either. Just like you told me before." The conversation offered them both a fragile comfort.

Needing space, Thalía changed hotel rooms to remain unseen, and kept her bruises hidden beneath scarves and makeup. She rested, allowed her body to heal, and slowly began to feel like herself again.

Once the marks on her face had faded, she returned to her old job at Elder Care, hoping to reclaim some normalcy. Luck had been on her side: the mentally ill client who had caused so many to quit had recently passed away, leaving a vacancy. She was welcomed back, her presence steady and professional, a quiet testament to her determination.

Two weeks passed, and Thalía worked hard to leave the violation behind. But one day, a sudden, burning discomfort in her private areas made it impossible to ignore reality. The pain grew unbearable, and fear began to creep in—not just of the illness, but of exposure and possible involvement with authorities.

She called Amy and explained the situation. Amy quickly gave her the details of an anonymous clinic that specialized in helping women in Thalía's situation, where personal anonymous.

Thalía acted immediately. The clinic tested her and confirmed what she had feared: she had contracted two Sexually Transmitted Disease's (STD)—gonorrhea and chlamydia, a result of her assault. Though the diagnosis was jarring, the treatment was swift, professional, and anonymous. The clinic treated her best they could, and for the first time in weeks, Thalía felt a flicker of relief.

It wasn't just about healing her body, it was about reclaiming control, step by careful step, over a life that had been forced into chaos. And with that relief came a renewed, quiet determination: she would survive, she would heal, and she would find a way to move forward.

CHAPTER 50

Picking up the Pieces

The days after the clinic visit were quiet but charged with an unspoken determination. Thalía returned to her room each night and allowed herself small rituals of normalcy: making tea, writing in her notebook, listening to music, and occasionally calling Amy, not to complain, but just to hear a familiar, caring voice.

Physically, her body was recovering, but the psychological scars ran deep. She found herself startled by sudden noises, flinching at shadows, and sometimes waking in the middle of the night drenched in sweat, memories of Jerry and his men clawing back into her mind.

To regain control, Thalía began setting strict routines for herself. She exercised in the mornings, went to work without fail, and slowly started to explore safer social spaces during the day. Each small decision, walking a new route, eating in public, buying herself something small, felt like reclaiming ownership over her life.

One afternoon, while cleaning an elderly client's home, she caught her reflection in a mirror and paused. After weeks of trembling, she remained unshaken. She saw a young woman who had survived horrors most couldn't imagine, and for a moment, she allowed herself to feel proud.

Amy remained her anchor. Though she occasionally pushed boundaries in her own way, Amy never pressured Thalía again. Their calls were lighter now, peppered with laughter and old jokes, allowing Thalía to remember that connection didn't have to come with fear. Amy encouraged her to take small steps toward independence, suggesting ideas like enrolling in night classes, saving her earnings, and reconnecting with her few safe friends.

For Thalía, independence wasn't just about escaping danger, it was about reclaiming her own choices. She set aside money from her Elder Care job, hidden in a small envelope under the mattress, each bill a small token of progress and self-reliance.

Most nights, she allowed herself to dream. Not dreams of escape, not fantasies of revenge—but simple, quiet hopes: one day, finding her cousin again, returning home to Honduras, and building a life that felt hers alone. Each night she whispered into the darkness, I am stronger than I think. I will make it through this.

It was slow work, the kind that required patience and courage, but Thalía realized she didn't just want to survive, she wanted to live.

And living, she knew, would mean facing the past on her own terms, not under anyone else's control.

CHAPTER 51

Echoes of the Heart

The year was 1991. About six months had passed since Thalía's tragic incident, and she had settled into a routine, steady life at twenty years old. She maintained her job at Elder Care, a position that came with a small studio apartment on the compound, a rare comfort and independence she had fought hard to achieve. Being on call wasn't ideal, but it allowed her to make enough money to support herself and keep her life in balance.

Part of the job's requirements included frequent blood tests every six months. Thalía, except for a slight cough, had been feeling perfectly healthy, so when Monday rolled around, she didn't expect anything out of the ordinary. She went in for her routine test, and by Wednesday, she received a call that would change her world.

The clinic informed her she needed to come back immediately to retest because her blood had tested positive for something of great concern. Panic gripped her. Thoughts raced through her mind, was it cancer? Leukemia? Something else entirely?

At the clinic, the doctor broke the news: her blood had tested positive for HIV. Thalía had barely heard of the virus and didn't know what it meant. She was told not to panic; they would run another test to confirm and rule out any errors.

Shaken, she immediately called Amy to share the news. Amy, equally unfamiliar with HIV, quietly researched the disease. She worried deeply about telling Thalía too much, afraid of adding to the young woman's burdens.

Despite her own fears, Thalía found solace in her connection with Cynthia. She called the diner to keep her updated about her life, letting Cynthia know she had steady work and a place to live. Cynthia was immensely proud of her resilience and independence.

That evening, Thalía visited the diner, hoping to gain some wisdom and comfort from Cynthia. The sight of her brought Cynthia joy, and she embraced Thalía warmly. "Sit down," Cynthia said, her voice tinged with both warmth and gravity. "I have some important news to share."

Thalía smiled softly. "And so do I," she said, hesitant to reveal her own frightening news.

As the diner closed for the night, Cynthia prepared a small meal for Thalía. The comforting aroma filled the quiet space. But soon, Cynthia's expression darkened. She shared the devastating news: she had been diagnosed with Stage-4 cancer and the Doctors were uncertain of how much longer she had to live. Despite her attempts, she had been unable to reconnect with her daughter, Cheney. Cynthia wanted to make amends before it was too late. She hoped to leave the diner and her business to Cheney if she chose to accept it.

Thalía's heart ached. "I'm so sorry, Cynthia," she said softly. "You've been like a mother to me since I've been here. I wish I could help you find Cheney, but I don't know how."

Cynthia reached across the table, her hand trembling slightly. "There may be something you *can* do for me," she said. "I have Cheney's phone number. But if I call, she won't speak to me. Maybe if you try, if you tell her what's happening, she might listen. She might give me a chance to make amends."

Thalía nodded immediately. "Of course. Just write it down. I'll call her tomorrow at a reasonable time." The thought of helping Cynthia left her overwhelmed with both responsibility and hope. Cynthia embraced her, tears streaming, grateful beyond words.

Then Cynthia asked, a gentle smile breaking through the sorrow, "So… what's this news you said you had?"

Thalía shook her head and smiled faintly. "Never mind, Cynthia. Tonight, let's just focus on *your* news."

It had been a long while, but for the first time, amidst fear and uncertainty, Thalía felt a sliver of purpose, a chance to help someone she loved, even as she struggled with the shadows of her own life.

Poor Little Poor Girl

CHAPTER 52

Shattered Truths

Early the next morning, Thalía returned to the clinic. The sterile white walls, the faint smell of antiseptic, the hum of fluorescent lights, all of it felt oppressive. The doctors confirmed what she had feared: she had contracted HIV!

They handed her pamphlets, explained the gravity of the disease, and stressed the seriousness of her prognosis. Death, they said, was a real and looming possibility.

Thalía didn't respond. Her knees buckled. She burst into tears, and before anyone could say another word, she stormed out of the clinic.

For a fleeting moment, she wanted to call Amy, to seek comfort, but she stopped herself. She knew exactly how she had contracted the virus: the assault by Jerry's goons. Rage coursed through her veins! The injustice of it all, the cruelty of the world, became too much!

Back in her room, she began throwing her belongings in a frenzy, each object a target for her anger. Clothes flew, papers scattered, lamps toppled. For over five relentless minutes, she vented her fury in utter hysteria, until exhaustion took over and she collapsed on the floor. She cried until she had no more tears.

As her vision cleared, her eyes fell on a photograph that had slipped from her belongings. A younger Amy, smiling warmly, standing beside a woman who looked eerily familiar, like Cynthia from the diner. Recognition struck her like a lightning bolt. She must have grabbed some of Amy's things that night she had to rush from the apartment when Jerry was there.

She stared at the photo, piecing it together. The woman in the picture, Amy's mother, looked very similar to Cynthia. Memories flickered—the day Cynthia had called Amy's phone, Amy's surprised reaction, the question: "How did you get this number?" The pieces were starting to click. Cynthia was Amy's mother... and Amy was Cheney!

Thalía's hands shook as she scrambled for the slip of paper that Cynthia gave her of Cheney's phone number. Heart hammering, she dialed the number with a blocked caller ID. The voice that answered, sharp and familiar, was unmistakable. Amy and Cheney—They were the same person!

This new finding shock and paralyzed her. The realization hit with full force: Amy—Cheney—was Cynthia's daughter! All along, the two had been separated, and now it was Thalía's responsibility to bring them together, to fulfill Cynthia's dying wish.

The next day, Thalía steeled herself. She had to tell Amy, had to explain everything: what she had uncovered, and her own devastating diagnosis. When Amy arrived at her room, the weight of the truth hung between them.

Thalía's voice trembled as she spoke. "Amy... I tested positive for HIV. Twice. The prognosis... it's serious. Death is imminent."

Amy's face went pale. She sank into a chair, tears spilling over, and Thalía sat beside her. They wept together, each feeling the enormity of the news.

Thalía tried to steady herself. "It's okay," she said softly. "My life's been hard. I didn't expect it to get any easier. Society... it doesn't give much hope to **poor little girls** like me."

Amy could only nod, her own voice caught in her throat. She knew Thalía was right.

Thalía drew a shaky breath and looked her friend straight in the eyes. "This is going to sound crazy, but… even though this news is devastating, I have… more news. And it's just as bad."

Amy blinked, stunned. "I don't know if I can handle anymore, what could possibly be worse than this?"

* * *

The Truth Unfolds...

Thalía took a deep breath, her voice trembling slightly. "Amy… remember the lady at the diner I've been telling you about sometimes?"

Amy nodded cautiously. "Yes…"

Thalía spoke slowly, deliberately, as if measuring each word. "Well… her name is Cynthia."

The weight of the words hit Amy immediately. The realization settled over her like a heavy, sudden wave. Cynthia, the woman Thalía had confided in, the warm, protective figure who had looked out for her all this time, was her own mother. Her heart raced, and a surge of emotion—anger, confusion, and guilt—flared up inside her.

"Why… why didn't you tell me this all this time?" Amy demanded, her voice edged with frustration.

Thalía reached out, trying to calm her. "Amy… I didn't put the pieces together myself until last night. You were using the name Amy instead of your real name, Cheney. I only realized it when I saw the picture of you and your mother after I… wrecked the room."

Amy froze, then looked down, recognizing the picture she had been searching for in vain.

Thalía continued gently, "The simple fact that you kept that picture... it means you still have some feelings for the relationship with your mother. You want it to matter. And now... I have to tell you more bad news."

Amy's chest tightened. "What is it?"

Thalía's voice softened, almost breaking. "Your mother... she's been trying to contact you because she has terminal cancer. The doctors... they've given her about one year to live."

The words hit Amy like a physical blow. Her eyes widened, tears immediately forming. The weight of lost time, of opportunities wasted, pressed down on her. Anger toward her mother mingled with a deep, aching sorrow. She couldn't yet bring herself to forgive her, but the urgency of the situation began to seep in. She had to act, before it was too late.

Thalía continued, her voice steady but filled with compassion. "She loves you, Amy. She realizes her mistakes... and she's been trying to make amends for as long as she could, but you didn't give her the chance."

Amy slumped back, taking a shuddering breath. "Wow... what a... what a fucking day," she murmured, her voice thick with emotion. "I just... I need to go home, sleep on this, and decide what to do tomorrow."

Thalía nodded, understanding. She reached out and squeezed Amy's hand gently. "Take all the time you need... but remember, it's never too late to make things right."

Amy didn't answer. She just let the words sink in, staring at the floor, knowing that tomorrow would bring decisions that could change everything.

CHAPTER 53

Reunited at Last

The following day, Cheney was a bundle of nerves. The thought of confronting her mother Cynthia, after all these years made her stomach churn. Thalía, sensing her friend's hesitation, gently encouraged her to go through with it.

"You should go see her in person," Thalía said. "I'll come with you for support if you want. I'll sit over at the corner table where she usually has me sit," she added with a small laugh. "After all, she always feeds me, and I could use a good meal."

Cheney smiled weakly but remained hesitant as the cab pulled up to the diner. The two girls lingered by the side door, out of sight. Thalía placed a hand on Cheney's arm.

"Time is precious, you know," she said softly. "Your mom's time is limited. You're already here. Just take a deep breath and go in."

Cheney nodded. "You're right, Thalía." With a steadying breath, she pushed the door open and stepped inside.

The bell above the door chimed, and Cynthia looked up, unaware of who had entered. "Welcome to Cynthia's! I'll be right with you," she called, moving toward them.

Thalía followed just behind Cheney. As Cynthia approached, her eyes fell on the girl in front of her. Recognition hit immediately.

The dishware slipped from her hands and crashed to the floor, "Cheney?!" she cried, tears streaming down her face.

Cheney froze, then ran into her mother's arms. Their embrace was long and passionate, a reunion filled with years of longing. Cynthia kept repeating, through tears, "Oh my baby, my beautiful baby! How I've missed you so! Thank you for coming back to me!"

After a while, Cynthia turned to Thalía, smiling through tears. She pulled her into a warm embrace. "Thank you so much for making this happen. Thank you for bringing my daughter back to me."

The other customers in the diner had paused to watch the reunion, clapping in celebration of the long-awaited moment. Cynthia raised her hands and addressed them.

"Thank you all," she said, her voice quivering. "But I'm closing the diner early today. This is my daughter, whom I haven't seen in years, and we need time to catch up."

The customers understood. They gathered takeout boxes and quietly left. Cynthia flipped the open sign to closed, signaling a rare private moment.

She guided Thalía to her usual corner table, serving her a warm meal, then walked across the diner to sit with Cheney. Mother and daughter talked for hours, apologizing for past misunderstandings and vowing to cherish whatever time they had left together.

Cynthia took Cheney's hands gently. "I want you to move in with me," she said. "I want to spend every moment I have left with you. I'll need your help as my condition worsens, and I want to be near you."

Cheney nodded, holding back tears. "I want that too. But I'll need a few days to take care of some business with… Jerry."

Cynthia asked and offered, "who is that, your boyfriend"? "You could even bring him along. We could all be one happy family!"

Cheney glanced at Thalía, who gave her a knowing smile. "No," Cheney said quietly. "That's definitely not gonna happen."

Cynthia laughed softly. "Well, suit yourself. As long as I have you with me, I'm happy."

Thalía beamed, relieved. Cheney would finally be free from Jerry, safe with her mother, and beginning a new chapter. Her future was bright—reunited with family, with the possibility of taking over the diner, and surrounded by love and support.

CHAPTER 54

The Wake-Up Call

The year was 1991, and the world was shaken by shocking news. On November 7th, Danny "Fanatic" Thompson, the star basketball player for the Los Angeles Vaders, publicly announced that he had contracted the HIV virus. A couple of weeks later, on November 24th, Teddie Furi, the legendary lead singer of the band Kingz, succumbed to AIDS.

Thalía, sitting in her small studio apartment, watched the events unfold on TV, her heart pounding. The stories dominated the news, flashing across every channel and front page. She was shocked, someone of Fanatic Thompson's fame, fortune, and talent had contracted the virus. Teddie Furi, whose music had touched millions, had died from it. The realization hit her with brutal clarity: this disease did not discriminate. Rich or poor, famous or unknown, no one was safe. And for her, a young woman living with HIV, the news was terrifyingly personal.

A few days later, Thalía walked through downtown, the crisp air mingling with the city's usual hum of traffic and chatter. She noticed a growing crowd outside a store, all eyes glued to a TV screen. Curiosity piqued, she edged closer and watched as the clip replayed: Fanatic Thompson, composed yet solemn, explaining his diagnosis to the world. The crowd murmured, shocked and uneasy, realizing the seriousness of the disease.

Thalía felt her stomach tighten. This was no longer an abstract fear. HIV was real, it was deadly, and it was her reality. Her mind raced as she thought of her own condition, contracted during the horrific assault by Jerry's goons. Every headline, every report, every word felt like a countdown.

Determined to understand her situation, Thalía, with Amy's support, dove into research. They scoured books, newspapers, and early medical publications, hoping to find a sliver of hope—a treatment, a cure, anything. The findings were grim. HIV, once contracted, led to AIDS, a near-certain death sentence in a matter of years, months, or even weeks; depending on how long the disease has been in the body untreated.

To make matters worse, news of Teddie Furi's death sent another shockwave across the globe. He had not even known he had the virus until it was too late. The world responded with fear, grief, and urgent action. Governments ramped up research, and public awareness campaigns began in earnest. The disease, once thought to affect only certain groups, was now recognized as a universal threat.

For Thalía, the news was both a warning and a wake-up call. She understood now more than ever the seriousness of her condition. She had limited time, and every day became precious. The awareness of the virus, the sudden losses of global icons, and the relentless media coverage forced her to confront the harsh reality: her life, as she had known it, would never be the same.

Yet, amid the fear and uncertainty, there was a resolve forming in Thalía. She would not let the disease define her. She would live each day with purpose, awareness, and courage, facing the future as bravely as she could, however uncertain it might be.

Desperate, she even found herself thinking about what Eleanor and all her many grandmas had said. She wondered if she should start changing her toothbrush every week, that maybe it would stop the virus from lingering in her body.

But then she snapped back to reality and told herself, *"Don't be silly, this is no common cold or the flu, this disease surely could not be cleared that easily."*

CHAPTER 55

A Flicker of Hope

Although just over twenty, Thalía had a soul that felt much older. The weight of everything she had endured—loss, trauma, betrayal, and now illness had left her spirit battered and weary. Some days, she wondered what she had done to deserve so much pain. At night, she prayed to God with trembling hands, begging Him to take away the suffering. She went to church often, hoping for peace, or at least a sign that her life wasn't cursed.

Despite her strength and resilience, depression had taken hold of her heart in a way that even Cheney couldn't break through. Thalía spent her days sitting in silence, lost in thought, her once lively eyes now dulled by sorrow. "If I wasn't so poor, I hate being poor" she would mutter, "I wouldn't be in this situation. Everything bad that's happened to me is because I was born poor with nothing."

She was angry, angry at the world, at society, at fate itself. Her voice trembled one afternoon as she said to Cheney, "Up until I was eleven, life was hard, but I could still find peace. Since twelve, everything has just gotten worse. I was ripped away from my cousin, sold into sex-trafficking, dragged from my home country, forced into hell—and now I'm going to die!"

Then came the words that pierced Cheney's heart like a knife. Thalía looked up, her voice hollow, and whispered, "Maybe I should just end it all now... so I don't have to endure any more pain."

Cheney's chest tightened. She knew Thalía had every reason to feel broken, but she couldn't, wouldn't, let her friend fall apart. Taking Thalía's trembling hands, Cheney spoke gently but firmly. "Listen to me. You've come too far to give up now. Think about Marco, your cousin. You've always told me how much he meant to you. If you're gone, who's going to find him? You're his light, Thalía."

Tears filled Thalía's eyes as Cheney continued, "And your father... you said he gave his life to save yours. You know he's watching you from heaven, and he wouldn't want you to quit. He'd want you to fight."

Cheney reminded her of the good she had brought into others' lives, how she'd helped reunite Cheney and Cynthia, giving mother and daughter the gift of time before Cynthia's illness took her. "You made that happen," Cheney said softly. "You gave me my mother back. You have a purpose, Thalía. And you have to keep believing that the doctors and scientists will find a cure. You're going to live to see it."

After a moment of silence, Cheney forced a smile and added jokingly, "Besides, there's no way in hell you're leaving me to run that Diner all by myself!"

Thalía let out a small laugh through her tears. Her laughter, long absent, returned, a delicate spark that brought life to the room—a flicker of faith that maybe, just maybe, she still had something to live for.

* * *

A New Dawn...

The morning sun filtered softly through Thalía's small apartment window, casting a warm glow over the room. Weeks of suffocating and despair faded as she woke lighter than before. Cheney had stayed with her late into the night, speaking words of hope, reminding her of her purpose—and, somehow, it had worked.

Thalía sat up in bed, letting the light wash over her face. Her body still ached from the scars of her past, and the shadow of HIV still loomed over her. Yet, she discovered a spark of determination she hadn't felt before. She realized that even if her time was uncertain, she could still choose how she lived it.

After a quiet breakfast with Cheney, Thalía decided to return to the Diner. Cynthia had been pleased to see her, and Thalía wanted to be near her, to continue helping where she could, and to feel connected to something positive. The scent of fresh coffee and warm bread welcomed her, grounding her in the familiar comfort of the place she had grown to love.

As she wiped down tables and served customers, her thoughts drifted to Marco. The cousin she had lost so many years ago, whose memory had been a guiding light through her darkest times. She hadn't heard any news of him recently, and yet the idea of finding him again filled her with a quiet resolve. She would live—live for Marco, for Cynthia, for Cheney, and for herself.

Poor Little Poor Girl

CHAPTER 56

Fury Unleashed

Thalía planned to meet Cheney at her old apartment to help her move her things before Jerry discovered her intentions. She approached the bottom of the stairwell, but suddenly, a loud commotion erupted from inside Cheney's apartment.

Her heart sank. Jogging up the stairs, a look of concern etched across her face, she heard a guttural male shout and the unmistakable sound of something breaking. The voice—deep, angry, and all too familiar, sent chills down her spine. Jerry. Somehow, he had found out.

Thalía's face hardened with determination. She pounded on the door, yelling, "Cheney! Open up!"

A voice screamed back from inside.

"Please, go get help! He's going to kill me!"

Jerry's voice cut through, venomous. "Fuck off, bitch! Or you're next!"

Fear surged through her, heart hammering in her chest. She realized that by the time she ran for help, Cheney might not survive. Fury and adrenaline fused into a single, reckless resolve.

She stepped back, wound her leg, and kicked the door with all her strength. It held. She kicked again—harder this time, and the door slammed open, swinging violently against the wall.

Inside, the scene froze her in place: Cheney lay on her back, Jerry straddling her. His left hand gripped her hair, pinning her down, and his right fist raised, ready to strike.

Without hesitation, Thalía charged.

Jerry spun around, catching sight of her just in time. He grabbed her mid-run and hurled her into the bottom edge of the kitchen counter. Pain exploded through her ribs as they slammed against the hard surface, but she refused to stay down.

Jerry advanced, fists raised, confidence radiating from every movement.

"Oh, you want some too, huh? Two-for-one special," he sneered, a cruel smirk on his face.

Blood trickled from Thalía's lip, but adrenaline sharpened her mind. She drew a slow breath, recalling Eleanor's lessons, the moves she had practiced a thousand times in secret. Her body trembled, but she was ready.

Shaky, bruised, but unbroken, she squared up to face him. Fury burned in her eyes.

It was now or never.

* * *

The Dynamic Battle...

Jerry swings a brutal looping punch meant to end her.

Thalía ducks just in time and drives her foot hard into his groin.

Jerry grunts, doubling over. Behind him, Cheney—bloodied, trembling—roars in defiance and leaps onto his back, clawing at his face.

Thalía (yelling): "Hold him! Hold him!"

Jerry thrashes violently, slamming his back into the wall. The impact crushes Cheney, but she clings tighter, fingers gouging at his eyes.

Thalía dives for the kitchen drawer, yanking it open and snatching a knife.

Jerry bucks Cheney off, sending her crashing into the floor. He turns, just as Thalía slashes across his chest. The cut isn't deep, but blood splatters across his shirt.

JERRY (snarling, spitting blood): "You're dead. BOTH of you!"

He lunges and connects a vicious punch to Thalía's face. Her head snaps sideways—the colored contact in one eye flies out as her nose bursts with blood. Dizzy, she spins and collapses against the counter.

Jerry turns toward Cheney, who's crawling for a weapon.

Through the haze, Thalía blinks, dazed.

Then, a memory flashes.

Eleanor's voice, clear and sharp in her mind:

"If you can't beat 'em clean... beat 'em dirty."

Her hand lands on a shard of broken glass from the shattered coffee table. Gritting her teeth, Thalía launches herself forward and drives the jagged edge into Jerry's kidney.

He howls, twisting and collapsing to one knee.

Cheney, shaking with fury, staggers upright and snatches a broken broomstick from the floor.

Jerry roars, swinging wildly. Thalía drops low and kicks the side of his knee, the joint buckles.

Cheney swings the broomstick like a bat. It cracks across Jerry's face with a sickening sound. Blood sprays.

Thalía (panting): "Now, Cheney!!"

Thalía lunges, wrapping her arms around Jerry's neck in a desperate chokehold. He thrashes, throwing wild elbows, one smashes across her ribs—but she doesn't let go.

Cheney charges again, screaming, and plunges the jagged end of the broomstick into his side.

Jerry's scream fills the room—raw, guttural, inhuman. He falls to one knee, blood pouring from his wound.

Thalía (straining): "Don't let him get up!"

Jerry, in a last surge of rage, flings Thalía off him. She crashes into the couch, gasping for air. He rips the broomstick from his side, blood gushing, and tosses it away.

He grabs Cheney by the throat, lifting her halfway off the ground.

But Thalía, driven by pure adrenaline, springs up and kicks him square in the bleeding wound. He staggers. She punches the same spot—again and again—

Left, right, left, right, left, right!

Each hit drives deeper until blood pours freely down his torso.

Jerry falters, eyes wide and glassy. Cheney, coughing and shaking, spots the knife on the floor.

Without hesitation, she grabs it, and drives it into his chest. Once! Twice!! Three times!!!

Jerry's mouth opens, soundless. He stumbles back, arms weakly reaching for help that won't come, collapsing onto the shattered coffee table. A crack. A gasp. Then stillness. . . . . Silence.

The only sounds are their gasping breaths and the dripping water from the broken sink.

Thalía and Cheney stare at each other, bloody, bruised, trembling—yet alive.

Jerry twitches once more, lets out a final gurgled breath... and goes limp.

Blood spreads across the floor, dark and thick, reflecting the flicker of the broken lamp.

Thalía lowers the knife, hands shaking.

* * *

Aftermath...

Thalía staggers over to the kitchen counter and grabs a few paper towels. Sits down on the floor with her knees to her chest, wiping blood from her face.

Cheney stands over Jerry's body, chest heaving, face blank.

Thalía (hoarse) You good?

Cheney doesn't answer. She drops the knife with a clang and walks slowly over to Thalía.

Thalía (voice shaking) You okay?

CHENEY (spitting blood) No. But I'm not dead.

They both just sit there on the floor, backs against each other, staring at Jerry's lifeless body.

Thalía says, "we're in big trouble". Cheney says, no way, it was self-defense. It was either him or us!

She says, but do you think the police will believe us?! We really fucked him up!

They sat there back-to-back, broken yet undefeated, they finally felt a small measure of safety as they leaned against each other.

As they sit, Cheney says "I wonder why hasn't anyone called the police yet?" *In a weird moment, they both breathe a hard sigh of relief and laugh off their victory.*

CHAPTER 57

The Ride Out

After that brief moment of stillness, reality hit like a sledgehammer.

Cheney's heart pounded so hard it hurt. The smell of blood still clung to the air, metallic and thick.

All she could think about was getting out. Out of this apartment. Out of this nightmare.

"Thalía," she gasped, "we need to go. I have to tell my mom what happened, she'll know what to do."

Thalía nodded, trembling. "Yes, let's call a cab and get out of here."

Cheney snapped her head around, panicked. "No! We can't call a cab. They'll have a record—time, pickup, everything. If they find Jerry..." She couldn't even finish the thought. "No one can know we were here."

Thalía blinked, swallowing hard. "Do you even know how to drive?"

Cheney looked at her. "You?"

Thalía hesitated. "I don't have a license, but I can drive well enough to get us to your mom's diner."

Cheney glanced around the wrecked apartment. "We don't have a car."

Thalía looked down at Jerry's body, motionless on the floor.

Cheney's face hardened. "He does."

She crouched beside Jerry, forcing herself not to gag at the sight of him, and unclipped the blood-streaked car keys from his belt loop. "We'll take his car and ditch it later. Right now, we just need to get the hell out of here."

Thalía opened her mouth to protest, but Cheney cut her off. "I can't drive anyway, I hurt my hand in the fight. I can't even grip the wheel."

Thalía took the keys, nodding. "Then I'll get us there."

Moments later, they were in Jerry's car—a white, older model Mercedes, pulling out of the complex. The night air was heavy, their minds spinning.

As they sped away, sirens wailed in the distance, growing louder, headed straight toward Cheney's building.

Cheney looked back through the rear window. "Ohhh... *now* someone calls them?" she muttered with a half-crazed smirk.

Thalía didn't reply, eyes locked on the road, trying not to shake. Every red light felt like a spotlight. Every turn felt too sharp, too loud, too dangerous.

They drove in tense silence for several blocks before stopping at a light near a gas station. Cheney's nerves were shot. "Pull over," she said suddenly. "I need a cigarette."

Thalía's knuckles tightened on the wheel. "Cheney, that's not a good idea. We're covered in blood. We're in *his* car."

"I won't go inside," Cheney insisted. "There's a machine by the side of the building. I'll be quick."

The light turned green.

Flustered, Thalía made a hard left, without realizing the oncoming car had the right of way.

Tires screeched. Horns blared. The other driver swerved, missing them by inches. "Watch where you're going bitch!" he shouted out his window.

Thalía froze. And as if fate wanted to twist the knife, a patrol car that had been idling nearby flicked on its lights and siren with a sharp *chirp*.

"Oh, God..." Thalía whispered.

Cheney went pale. "Keep calm. Just, just keep calm."

They pulled into the gas station parking lot, hearts pounding. The officer stayed in his cruiser for a moment, running the plates. His brow furrowed when the name *Jerry Dalton* flashed on his screen.

Then his radio crackled:

"Be on the lookout for two female suspects, possibly driving a white Mercedes, older model. Connected to a homicide near..."

The officer's eyes shot up to the car in front of him.

He approached slowly, one hand near his holster. "License and registration, please."

Thalía's voice shook. "I—I don't have a license."

He leaned in, eyes scanning the interior. Blood. On their hands. On their clothes.

"Step out of the vehicle," he ordered, pulling his gun as his voice turned firm. "Now!"

Thalía froze. Cheney raised her trembling hands, whispering, "It was self-defense..."

"Step. Out. Of. The. Car."

Backup arrived moments later, sirens blaring, lights flashing blue and red across the gas station walls.

The two girls didn't fight. Didn't run. Didn't speak.

They knew. It was over.

As they were cuffed and led toward the patrol car, Cheney looked back at Thalía, both of them blood-streaked, exhausted, hollow-eyed.

Cheney (quietly): "We're not bad people... we just... didn't have a choice."

The officer didn't respond.

The door closed. The cruiser pulled away, its lights fading into the night.

Behind them, the gas station neon flickered, buzzing like a broken memory.

* * *

At the Station...

The air was thick with disinfectant and despair.

Fluorescent lights buzzed overhead, bleaching the color out of everything, including Thalía's hope.

When they lined her up for her mugshot, she had no idea how significant that photo would become.

One of Jerry's punches had knocked out her colored contact, leaving her natural mismatched colored eyes exposed.

Click.

The flash went off, freezing her heterochromia in natural color. That single image would travel farther than she could ever imagine.

She was worried that the incident with Mr. Neymore would surface, but finally she had one stroke of luck, as it never did.

* * *

The Call for Help...

The moment Cheney was allowed a phone call, she dialed her mother with shaking hands.

"Mom... please, it's bad. I need you."

Cynthia's voice on the other end was calm but urgent. "Where are you?"

Within hours, Cynthia arrived at the station, a familiar face among the local officers. She was respected in the community, most of the men had eaten at her diner at one time or another.

They knew her reputation, her kindness. They listened.

She pleaded her daughter's and Thalía's case, explained what happened.

Self-defense. A history of abuse.

And by the next morning, Cheney was out on bail. Pale, silent, trembling—but free.

* * *

Undocumented...

Thalía wasn't so lucky.

No ID. No family in the country. No papers to prove who she even was.

The Police Officer asked her, "Why are you in America without papers?"

Thalía lifted her chin, and replies with heartfelt emotion. *"**Not everyone who is in America, wants to BE in America, some were brought here against their will**"*!

The Police Officer felt where she was coming from and could only nod in agreement.

When they asked what country she came from, she told them everything; the trafficking, the abuse, being brought to America against her will, and her desperate attempts to reach her cousin Marco in Honduras.

The officers exchanged uneasy looks. Some pitied her. Others just saw a problem they didn't want to deal with.

Due to the severity of the charge, law enforcement had to contact Honduran authorities.

Within days, her mugshot—that haunting image of her mismatched eyes, was plastered across news broadcasts in both the U.S. and Europe, and South America.

"Unidentified woman involved in fatal altercation in Miami Florida," the headlines read.

Thalía didn't understand any of it; the laws, the process, the bureaucracy.

All she knew was that she and Cheney had done the same thing, but only one of them got to walk free.

* * *

Jail...

Jail was a nightmare she hadn't been prepared for.

Guards were cruel, impatient. Some mocked her accent. Others stared too long.

The inmates were worse, jealous of her looks, fascinated by her eyes.

A few called her "witch eyes."

Others tried to touch her, whispering things in the dark.

When one woman cornered her in the showers, Thalía snapped.

She broke the woman's nose in a single punch.

The guards dragged her away screaming and threw her into isolation.

After days of tension, she could finally breathe. The silence was heavy, but peaceful.

No one to touch her. No one to threaten her. Just concrete walls and her own thoughts.

* * *

Jerry's Criminal Background...

Meanwhile, investigators dug deeper into Jerry's record.

What they found painted a very different picture,

Drug trafficking. Public drunkenness. Assaults. Even an open warrant for a homicide in another state.

Suddenly, the narrative shifted.

The DA's office began to reclassify the case.

Two young women with clean records. One known abuser with a violent record.

Evidence of a struggle.

A clear motive for self-defense.

And just like that, after days of confinement, silence, and fear—Thalía was released on bond, pending trial.

When she stepped out of the county jail, the morning air hit her face like freedom, cold, bright, and unreal.

She looked up at the sky, hand still trembling from everything she'd endured.

She didn't know what would happen next.

Only that she'd survived the worst… for now.

CHAPTER 58

The Flip: Rage, Fury, and Revenge

They opened the cell door to a world that felt both painfully familiar and utterly alien. The cold light of morning fell across Thalía like an accusation. For a heartbeat she simply stood there, the loose sleeves of her jail-issued shirt hung from arms, her face a map of bruises and sleepless nights.

They led her out. Paperwork signed. A guard's curt nod. Her freedom smelled like diesel and cheap coffee, like the city that had chewed her up and spat her out. She stepped into it deliberately, as if testing whether the ground would hold.

She did not call Cynthia. She did not call Cheney.

It wasn't spite. It was a last kindness.

Cynthia had stitched a life of fragile repairs with her hands; Cheney had a future finally steady enough to cradle. They deserved the warmth of that little bubble, the diner's clatter, the small laughter over coffee, the late-night mending of regrets, without Thalía's shadow falling over every sweet moment. If Cynthia's last year could be soft, let it be so. If Cheney could begin to breathe again, let her breathe. Thalía could not, in good conscience, be the storm that darkened their sky.

So she left them a note instead—two lines only, written with a shaky pen on a grocery receipt and tucked beneath a chipped salt shaker at Cynthia's usual table: I love you. Don't look for me. Live. She watched the diner door close behind her as if sealing the last good thing she'd known.

Aloneness settled in like a second skin. It had been a long companion in jail; now it walked beside her on the pavement, a co-conspirator in a plan that had nothing to do with hope. In isolation, hours had been skeletons to be filled. She had filled them with stone-cold truths: the world had no place for her softness; kindness had been a currency she could not spend; even the law, when it was finally on her side, had come too late, too clumsy. The jail's sterile solitude had distilled one clear thing, mercy was rare. Justice was slower still. If someone had to burn to get the light on, then she would be the match.

Rage arrived as a quiet, efficient intelligence. It was not the wild, empty fury that had almost cost her life in Jerry's apartment; this was something narrower, sharp, and particular. She did not want to flail. She did not want pointless violence for its own sake. She wanted ruin, not for the sake of spectacle, but for the sake of balance: the crooked men who trafficked, the buyers who sat safely in foreign hotels, the invisible ledger of names and bank transfers that had turned children into merchandise. She had watched too many faces look away. She had borne witness to the small, daily cruelties that made a trade in human bodies possible. That ledger (she thought) had a number, and numbers could be followed.

When the tinder of fury ignited, it didn't make her a villain so much as a relentless force. She vowed to hurt what hurt her: the network, the men who traded lives for profit, the complacent officials who closed their eyes. She would not be content with scraps of revenge thrown at the feet of a single predator. No. She would aim for the spine.

But she was not reckless. The months in that cold cell taught her patience. Patience could be weaponized. So could memory. She began to collect small things at first: the number of the truck that had taken them, the recall of João's emblem when she closed her eye and traced it on her palm, the cadence of a buyer's laugh remembered from the auction's darkened hall. She kept these like prayer beads, threading them into an obsession.

She did not only think of destruction. She thought of exposure. Names on paper. Men on record. Secrets made public. The idea of light was a kind of revenge, a brighter more bureaucratic fury: press, prosecutors, investigators who could not be bribed. She wanted them all to feel, in the cold precision of law and publicity, the humiliation and the helplessness they had dealt out so casually.

There was a softer, stranger edge to it: revenge for Thalía was a promise to herself and to Marco—a promise carved into the spine of a notebook she carried under her coat. She pulled the little photograph from the pocket, the one of them as kids with a battered ball between them, and touched it like a talisman. Finding Marco would not only be the undoing of some of that emptiness; it would be a ledger closed. It would announce, with blunt clarity, that they were not disposable.

She changed her face. Not with makeup or disguise, but with purpose. She dyed her hair darker, let it grow longer and loose until it hid the line of her cheeks that the cameras knew. She began to dress like a ghost in plain clothes, unremarkable and practical. She traded hand-to-hand violence for things that left no fingerprints: names she could look up, shipments she could watch, numbers that moved money. She read reports, listened at diner counters, befriended clerks who sold cigarettes, learned the routes of trucks at dawn. Each fact was a stitch in a net she intended to cast wide.

On the bruised underbelly of the city she became a student of patterns. She learned how the corridors of power hid themselves behind polite offices. She learned that mercy could be bought if you knew the ledger; and the ledger had a back door. She began to map that back door.

Rage without precision was a storm. Rage with precision was a plan.

In the nights that followed she slept in different rooms, on couches that smelled of other people's lives. She ate in diners that did not know her and left exact change on the table. She let the news play in the background, listening for any whisper of trafficking arrests, auctions broken up, raids that might mean a kind of distant, bureaucratic justice. The world kept turning, indifferent and loud, but under her skin something new had fastened itself like a hinge.

She did not know whether she would live long enough to see any of it through. The diagnosis burned at the edges of every decision, a clock that ticked and sang and told her that time was a commodity she had to spend like a weapon. Perhaps that is why the turn felt inevitable: with the end near, she could either waste what remained in quiet despair, or spend it making a difference that would hurt the people who thought themselves untouchable.

She kept one small mercy for herself: she would not burn everything to ash. She would not become what had taken her. There were lines she would not cross. There were faces she would not destroy without reason. Her anger had teeth, but it had rules. Those rules were as much about what she would not let be lost—the memory of her father's courage, the small kindnesses of Cynthia, the loyalty of Cheney when she could have walked away, as about what she would dismantle.

That evening she stood on a quiet bridge and watched the river pull the city lights into strips of trembling gold. The wind tugged at her hair. She pressed the photograph of Marco to her chest and whispered, not to anyone, not even to him: "If you are out there, find me this way."

Her voice went with the water.

When she walked away from the railing, she did so with the slow, sure step of someone who had chosen a course. Rage had become work. Fury had become method. Revenge had been tempered by direction.

She vanished into the city, less a woman than a promise set loose: a promise that those who had trafficked and profited would one day, quietly and publicly, be held to account. And if the law would not move fast enough, she would make sure the light did.

The hunt had begun.

CHAPTER 59

The Venomous Bait

Consumed by a blinding, righteous rage, Thalía returned to the path of corruption, but this time, her mission was cold and absolute: to intentionally spread the very sickness that had been brutally forced upon her. She carried the venom of her past, determined to use it as a weapon.

Dressed in provocative clothing that promised and exposed, she entered the harsh, neon glow of the Night Club. Attention found her immediately; three eager men swarmed her, competing to buy her a drink. Yet, their cheap enthusiasm only fueled her emptiness—they weren't the target. She scanned the hazy room until her eyes settled on her prey.

He was a loud, boorish man, clearly sloshed, who was currently pawing at the dancers, shouting obscenities, and escalating a pointless argument with the bouncers. He was trouble incarnate, demanding attention he hadn't earned.

A massive security guard stepped in, his face set hard. "I don't care who you are, lieutenant. Stop harassing the girls or you're out. Boss's orders or not!"

The man, bristling with false authority, shoved the guard's arm away. "I'm the damn man round these here parts, and besides my brother-in-law's the damn Mayor! One call, and I can have this whole damn establishment shut down!" "Now leave me the hell alone, I do what the hell I want!"

In a taunting manner, he yells, "WHAT, WHAT, get used to it!" (while walking away he yells) "That's what the hell I thought!"

The guard, past his breaking point, didn't address the drunkard but shouted toward the back office. "Boss! Why do you keep letting this pedophile in here? He chases off clients and scares the girls! Mayor's brother-in-law or not, he needs to go, or I'm walking!"

When the security guard spat the word "pedophile," a chilling certainty washed over Thalía. Her mission suddenly had a face, a name, and a twisted moral purpose. This wasn't just revenge; this was duty. He would not harm another child. This man was hers!

She moved, every step a predatory strut, knowing the man couldn't possibly resist the confident, focused attention. He watched her approach, his glazed eyes widening in genuine awe, the argument forgotten. Before she even stopped, his arm was around her waist, pulling her close.

"Well, how you doin', baby?" he slurred.

The security guard started toward them, his mouth open to intervene, but Thalía gave a swift, dismissive wave. "No, no. It's fine," she said, her voice smooth and convincing.

"How you doing Lieutenant?" She says in a flirtyful way. After a few minutes of superficial conversation and two quickly downed drinks, she leaned close enough for him to smell her perfume and whispered, "Let's get out of here. Your place."

His face split into a triumphant, bloated grin. He eagerly agreed, clutching her hand like a trophy as they moved toward the exit. "Fuck all y'all bitches!" he bellowed back at the crowd, drunk on cheap liquor and what he mistakenly believed was a conquest. "I got the baddest one in here, and she ain't even a damn stripper!" (laughing obnoxiously as they exited)

The apartment he took her to was the kind of place that smelled of rented power and things bought to impress without soul. He staggered to the bedroom, fumbling with a belt, muttering promises. Thalía walked the rooms, slow and steady, eyes sweeping like a trained investigator, hands light and deliberate. A dresser door stuck; a wallet half-hidden under a magazine; a business card under an ashtray; a list on a yellow sheet folded into a pocketbook—names, dates, times, and, crucially, a vehicle registration. Men who traffic and pay leave paper like breadcrumbs.

She had found the phone, fingerprint-smudged and unlocked, the predator's arrogance leaving it open and careless. She sent one message from his device to a number she had memorized from a different list earlier, a journalist she'd read about, someone who had gone after trafficking networks before. The message was naked and direct: Suspicious activity tonight. Evidence attached. Then she uploaded a photo from the dresser drawer—a snapshot of a ledger page, and hit send.

* * *

The Message...

Unlike before, when fear once ruled her, Thalía now felt nothing. The emptiness inside her had hardened into calm resolve, a void colder than steel. She went with the man to his room without hesitation, performing what needed to be done as though detached from her own body. There were no nerves, no tremors, just the mechanical rhythm of someone who had long since stopped caring about life or death.

In the wee hours of the morning, she slipped quietly out of bed. The man snored, heavy and oblivious. In the bathroom, under the faint buzz of a flickering light, she pulled out a tube of bright red lipstick. Twisting it open, she pressed the red stick to the mirror and scrawled a message in deliberate, jagged strokes.

When she was done, she looked at her reflection for a moment, not at her face, but at the emptiness behind her eyes. Then she turned away, leaving without a sound, the door clicking softly shut behind her.

The man awoke hours later to a strange stillness. The air felt colder than it should have, heavy with a metallic quiet. He sat up, rubbing his temples, trying to piece together the foggy blur of the night before. The perfume still hung in the air, sweet, unmistakably real. So it hadn't been a dream.

Grumbling, he swung his legs off the bed and shuffled toward the bathroom. The harsh light stabbed at his eyes when he flipped the switch, and then his breath caught.

Across the mirror, written in thick, red lipstick, were the words:

'Welcome to the disease that there is no cure for!'

For a moment, he could only stare, frozen. His heart pounded against his ribs, and the blood drained from his face. He wanted to believe it was a prank, a cruel joke—but something inside him, something instinctive, told him it wasn't.

The chill in the room deepened. His knees weakened as dread began to bloom in his gut, spreading like frost. Slowly, he backed out of the bathroom, eyes fixed on the words as though they might move if he looked away.

The sheets were tangled, from where she had lain. Her perfume lingered like a ghost, sweet, suffocating, impossible to ignore.

He stumbled back into the room, the silence now deafening, the realization crashing over him like a wave.

She was gone.

And she had left behind something far worse than an empty bed.

* * *

Mission Accomplished...

That was it, she had done it. She had followed through. The drunken pedophile was her first victim: an asshole who had thought he could use his status, buy anything and get away with it. Thalía had left him a message he would never forget, and something inside her unclenched.

But the release was fleeting. The city at night pulsed and breathed around her, neon and sirens and stray laughter blending into one long, aching hum. Thalía walked those streets like a ghost, moving between the glow of storefronts and the shadows behind alleyways. The nightlife in Miami was rugged and raw—a tangle of loneliness, hunger, and want—and she moved through it with a single, terrible clarity.

She wasn't hunting men at random. She scanned faces the way she once scanned the horizon at home: for signs, for telltale habits, for the way a man looked at a girl when he thought no one was watching. Her rage had a focus now, not merely self-destruction, but a river redirected. The thought that kept her feet moving was the same thought that had sustained her through every loss: vengeance for the children who never had a voice. For the boys and girls sold, hidden, erased. For the cousins and sisters and friends whose names would never make the papers.

There was a darkness to what she'd chosen, she knew that. She was no hero. She was broken, and she was dangerous. But the life had worn her down into a person who could walk into a crowded room and see pain in the way someone laughed too hard, in the way someone kept looking over their shoulders. Where others saw only business as usual, she saw culpability.

So she became deliberate. She watched. She waited. When opportunities presented themselves, she acted—swift, cold, efficient—a phantom judgement that left more questions than answers. Each act changed her a little: less frightened, more certain, and harder to stop.

Yet even as she moved through this new life, part of her still remembered softer things, the taste of childhood mangoes, the smell of rain on dirt roads, Marco's laugh. Those memories were knives that cut the same way vengeance did: they made her purpose beautiful and monstrous at once.

She knew the path she'd chosen had no clean end. There would be fallout; investigations, blood on other hands, people looking for answers where there were only shadows. She also knew she could not go back to the frightened girl who had hidden behind kitchen doors and prayed. That girl was gone.

So she walked on, seeing red, every step a promise to herself, to the lost, however dark the cost.

CHAPTER 60

Streetlight Judgment

The strip hummed with the same tired neon that had watched this corner of the city for years. Thalía drifted along the sidewalk and before long found herself in front of three girls who looked far too young to be out alone at night. She struck up small talk, easy questions at first, until curiosity pushed her to ask their ages.

"Why are you out here doing this?" she asked. "Shouldn't you be home, in bed, getting ready for school tomorrow?" "I can tell you guys are not even eighteen years old!"

One of the girls bristled. "Hold up, why you asking all these questions? You the police or something?"

They laughed, a high, nervous sound that tried to mask something else—pride maybe, or fear. They boasted about the cash they pulled in, how they made a week's pay that the teachers at school don't even make in a month. The light-skinned girl had a faded bruise shading her cheekbone; a recovering black eye that didn't match the laugh in her voice.

Thalía couldn't help but notice it. "What happened to your eye?" she asked.

"Nothin'," the girl said, shrugging like it was nothing at all. "I kinda messed up and my guy made sure I don't do it again. I'm good, though." The three of them giggled in the way of girls who've rehearsed toughness until it feels like a habit.

"When you say 'my guy,' you mean your pimp?" Thalía pressed.

"Don't worry about all that," the girl snapped. Another of them, bolder than the rest, turned to Thalía. "What you doin' out here? You look young too, and real pretty. I know you make a lotta money."

"Almost twenty-one," Thalía said. "I just started, and I kinda don't have much of a choice."

"Well, where's your pimp?" the bold one asked. "'Cause if my pimp catches you here talking to us, he's gonna kick your ass, and ours too. Get outta here before you get us all in trouble."

"So he beats you for stupid reasons," Thalía said, voice low. "And he knows you're underage, right?"

"Okay, that's enough," the light-skinned girl snapped, sudden and sharp. "This ain't 'a thousand questions' night. Mind your business and we'll mind ours. Now get outta here, before Tony comes."

"Tony?" Thalía began, but she didn't finish. A low roar of an engine cut her off as a sleek car slid into view.

The girls' bravado crumpled at once; their faces collapsed into fear. Thalía felt the cold tighten in her chest, but she kept her voice steady as she stepped forward and leaned in, speaking just above a whisper. "Don't worry. I got this."

* * *

I Got This...

As Tony approached, his voice cut through the night. "What the hell are y'all doing out here lollygagging with this bitch? Y'all supposed to be out here talking to Johns and making me my money!"

He shoved one of the girls roughly, and Thalía stepped forward without hesitation, placing herself between him and the girls. "No, Tony, it's not like that at all," she said quickly. "I asked them who the man was, and they told me about you, that you're the best pimp around these parts. I asked if I could talk to you because I want to work for you. They wouldn't give up your name or number because they were looking out for you... but here you are!"

Tony raised an eyebrow. "So how did you know my name then?"

Thalía kept her cool. "The girl just said it when you walked up," she replied.

Tony's lips curved into a slow, approving smile. "Okay, okay... you're pretty as hell. I could definitely use a girl like you on my team. You'd make me a lot of money."

He leaned in slightly. "One thing though... in order for you to be on my team, I gotta test you first, make sure you're good enough, if you know what I mean."

Thalía's lips curled into a sly, seductive smile. "Yes, Daddy. I know exactly what you mean," she said, her eyes locking onto his. "So... what are we waiting for? I'm ready right now."

Tony grinned wide. "Cool. Hop your fine ass in the car!"

As she opened the door, Thalía glanced back at the girls and gave them a knowing smile before sliding in and sitting down. The three of them watched her with a mixture of awe and admiration. The light-skinned girl finally spoke up, a grin spreading across her face. "Now that's a bad bitch right there."

All three of them laughed, the sound ringing out lightly over the neon-lit street.

* * *

Mirror and Gold...

The ride to Tony's place was short, but the silence between them was heavy, almost suffocating. The interior of his car reeked of expensive leather and cheap cologne, a strange mix that seemed to match him perfectly. Tony drove recklessly, weaving through Miami's neon-lit streets as if the city belonged to him, one hand firm on the wheel, the other casually resting on Thalía's thigh.

Thalía let out a soft, practiced laugh when he flirted, tilting her head just so, pretending shyness and eagerness. Submissive. Vulnerable. Everything he wanted to see. She fed the illusion perfectly, every movement calculated to keep him convinced she was just another girl he could control.

When they arrived at his condo, a flashy high-rise perched above the glowing city, Tony dragged her inside, his grip on her wrist a touch too tight. The interior was a spectacle of mirrors and gaudy gold fixtures, money flaunted in every corner. And yet, the place felt hollow, soulless. Just like him.

Inside his bedroom, Tony wasted no time asserting his authority. He barked orders like he was still on the streets, and Thalía played the part flawlessly. She obeyed, letting him believe he had conquered another girl. Every second of it made her stomach turn, but her face stayed blank, her mind locked on one thing: survival.

* * *

Calculated Desire...

Tony yanked Thalía toward him, his hands roaming with a greedy eagerness, a wide, predatory grin plastered across his face. Thalía returned a slow, sultry smile, letting her lips curve just enough to hide the disgust coiling inside her.

She let his hands wander while she subtly took control, slipping her fingers under the hem of his shirt and pulling it over his head in one fluid, practiced motion. His skin was warm beneath her touch, his breath quickening, but she remained calm, every movement measured, her mind focused on the game she was playing.

Thalía smiled—slow, dangerous, a curve that promised nothing but danger beneath the surface.

Tony approached with swagger, every step claiming ownership. His hands gripped her waist roughly, pulling her flush against him.

She tilted her head, exposing her neck, letting out a soft, breathy laugh that sounded like surrender—but was anything but.

It was all an invitation, a carefully crafted illusion. *Good,* she thought. *Let him believe he's already won.*

Leaning close, she whispered in his ear, her voice low, wicked, and full of unspoken intent,

"Show me what kind of man you are."

Tony pressed her against the wall, mouth crashing onto hers. Thalía kissed him back—deep, slow, measured, letting him feel in control while she steered every motion beneath the surface. Their bodies tangled, grinding together, heat rising like a warning.

He whispered filth and promises in her ear: wealth, protection, ownership. Thalía moaned softly, a sound perfected through practice, masking the cold calculation in her mind. Every movement was deliberate. Every kiss a lie. Every brush of skin a setup.

Tony lifted her effortlessly, carrying her to the bed as if she weighed nothing. Clothes fell away, breaths grew ragged. But in Thalía's mind, it wasn't passion, it was strategy. She scanned the room, memorizing every exit, every obstacle, every gleam of the metal knife on the nightstand. Just in case.

She gave him everything he wanted, or at least, everything he thought he wanted, while plotting his downfall with each passing second. When it was over, Tony lay back, smug and spent, the self-proclaimed master of a kingdom he didn't know was already crumbling beneath him.

"You're mine now, girl," he muttered, half-asleep, pride thick in his voice. "Gonna make me a rich nigga."

Just like before, in the middle of the night, Thalía made her move. The TV hummed softly, providing cover for her careful steps.

She slid from the bed with feline grace, naked skin gleaming under the dim light, mind sharp, cold, calculating. Her body ached with rage, but she buried it deep. Quietly, she grabbed her dress and mini-purse from the floor, tiptoeing toward the bathroom attached to his bedroom. Every step was measured, every movement a rehearsal in precision.

She pulled the bright red tube of lipstick from her mini-purse, twisted it open, and leaned close to the mirror. In bold, jagged letters, she scrawled:

'Welcome to the disease that there is no cure for!'

She held her reflection for a long, steady second. No tears. No fear. Only fire.

Before leaving, she retrieved a small, crumpled note she had written hours earlier, her contingency if the moment ever came. She slid it carefully under Tony's wallet on the nightstand. It read simply:

"You don't own anyone anymore."

Without a sound, Thalía slipped back into her dress, snatched her heels, and crept toward the front door, keeping each step measured, deliberate. She disappeared into the thick Miami night, shadows swallowing her whole.

She didn't look back. She didn't need to.

* * *

The Meltdown...

Tony woke hours later, sprawled across the rumpled bed, the heavy Miami air pressing down like a second skin.

After a night of indulgence, he instinctively reached for his nightstand, snatched some cocaine, and took a hit—unaware that Thalía had laced it with PCP from his own stash. The effects hit faster than he expected.

He stumbled toward the bathroom to relieve himself, only to notice the bed empty. *She must be freshening up,* he thought.

Then he saw it.

Across the bathroom mirror, jagged, angry letters screamed:

'Welcome to the disease that there is no cure for!'

Red streaks smeared down the glass, like blood.

The cocaine mixed with PCP tore through him. His heart hammered; his legs felt like jelly. Staggering, he gripped the sink for balance, staring into the mirror—into the face of a man who had just been played.

"Disease?" he muttered, the word thick in his throat.

Paranoid, he felt like his skin was itching, a deep, crawling sensation beneath the surface. Sweat poured from his forehead. His stomach twisted violently. He doubled over the sink, dry heaving. (Anyone looking from afar would laugh hysterically at this comical paranoid performance)!

The TV, previously subtle, now seemed that it blared at full volume: a news clip of Fanatic Thompson announcing he had contracted HIV. Panic slammed into him harder than any fist ever could.

Trembling, he grabbed his phone, dialing doctors, contacts, even shady street medics, but no one answered. The silence was deafening.

He ripped open drawers, tossing pill bottles, rubbing alcohol, anything he thought might fix what she had done. He scrubbed his skin raw, desperate to wash away the invisible poison.

And then the whispers began, crawling inside his mind:

You've been marked. You're poisoned. It's already inside you.

Memories of rumors he'd heard—girls set up, infected men on purpose, silent killers cloaked in beauty shredded his thoughts.

He stared at himself again, the mirror streaked with crimson lipstick, dripping like bleeding glass. Paranoia clawed at him: every joint ached with decay, every drop of sweat a sign of his body shutting down.

He stumbled back, knocking over the nightstand. The knife clattered to the floor, too late, useless.

Tony slowly sank to the cold tile, fear overtook his obnoxious courage, his empire of street power crumbling inside his mind. All of it, undone by one girl. One beautiful, clever, lethal girl.

And the worst part? He had no idea if it was real… or if she had simply shattered him from the inside out.

Tony would wake up to his empire beginning to rot, and he wouldn't even realize how or when it started.

* * *

Free, in Red…

The night air wrapped around Thalía like a velvet cloak. Miami pulsed beneath her—the hum of traffic, the low thump of music spilling from passing cars, the endless rhythm of a city that never slept. Her heels dangled from her fingers as she walked barefoot down the glowing strip, her steps light, deliberate, free.

Behind her, high above the city, Tony's world was unraveling, but Thalía didn't need to see it to know. She could feel it in the air, a shift, a release, the quiet power of justice done in whispers rather than screams.

She stopped at a crosswalk, catching her reflection in a storefront window. The lipstick was gone from her lips, but the fire in her eyes still burned. A small, knowing smile tugged at her mouth.

She reached into her purse, pulling out the same bright red lipstick—the weapon, the warning, the signature. With a slow, steady hand, she traced a single word onto the glass:

FREE.

The traffic light turned green. She slipped the lipstick back into her purse, stepped off the curb, and vanished into the flow of the city, one woman among millions, invisible yet unforgettable.

As Thalía crossed to the other side of the street, she spotted the three young girls under the glow of a flickering streetlight. A faint smirk touched her lips. She knew she'd done something incredible, Tony would never again have the chance to control them.

It was a slim hope, but she clung to it, that without his grip on their lives, maybe, just maybe, they'd find a way to become something more than what the streets had made them.

Somewhere far above, Tony was learning the cost of underestimating a woman who refused to be owned.

And Thalía?

She didn't look back.

She never would.

CHAPTER 61

The Politician

Thalía's next target was none other than Mayor Richard Finley, a man whose power masked a trail of corruption and sin. He was notorious for cheating on his wife, soliciting prostitutes, and, worst of all, preying on underage girls.

Despite multiple investigations and countless whispers behind closed doors, Finley always managed to slip through the cracks, shielded by the same system that was supposed to bring men like him to justice. His protection ran deep. He'd handpicked his police chief—an old friend and loyal enabler, and his brother-in-law a Lieutenant, ensuring that every accusation vanished before it could reach the light of day.

But Thalía had seen enough. This time, he wouldn't escape the consequences. Not with her watching. Not with her coming for him.

When Thalía learned that Mayor Finley would be attending a high-profile charity gala, she recognized the perfect opportunity. That night, she dressed to command attention, a vision of elegance and allure. Every detail was deliberate: the curve of her dress, the shimmer of her lipstick, the slow confidence in her stride. She didn't need to chase him; men like Finley always came to her.

The mayor spotted her almost instantly. Even with his wife standing dutifully at his side, he couldn't help himself—his eyes lingered, his smirk widening with every stolen glance. He whispered crude jokes to his entourage, his hand resting too long on the backs of young women who laughed nervously in response. His wife, impeccably dressed and heartbreakingly composed, stood there in silence, the pain in her eyes sharp and familiar.

For a fleeting moment, Thalía felt a pang of sympathy for the woman—trapped in humiliation, bound to a man who wore deceit like cologne. But she quickly brushed the feeling aside. Pity wouldn't serve her tonight. Justice would.

She glanced down at the table where her drink rested. A small event flyer lay beside it, glossy, pocket-sized, listing the contact emails and phone numbers of the key organizers. Among them were Mayor Finley's and his wife's. Without a second thought, Thalía folded the flyer neatly and slipped it into her purse. Instinct. Preparation. Just in case.

Throughout the evening, Finley's gaze kept drifting back to her. Thalía returned each look with a playful smile, a tilt of her head, a spark that promised danger disguised as desire. By the end of the night, his self-control had dissolved entirely.

He swaggered toward her, reeking of arrogance and expensive whiskey.

"Hi, beautiful," he drawled, his tone slick with entitlement. "What's your name?"

"Sonya," she lied smoothly, the name slipping off her tongue like silk.

They chatted briefly, meaningless small talk wrapped in false charm until he leaned closer, his grin widening. "Well, Sandra," he said, getting her name wrong without a hint of shame, "what are you doing this weekend?"

Thalía tilted her head, her voice a whisper of seduction.

"You," she said with a soft giggle.

Finley chuckled, pleased with himself. "You should come out with me on my boat, the lake, a few drinks… stars overhead. You'll love it."

She smiled, pretending to hesitate. "Hmm… sounds tempting."

"Perfect," he said quickly. "I'll send a car to pick you up."

Thalía's smile deepened—slow, knowing, dangerous.

"No need," she murmured. "Just give me the address. I'll find my own way."

And with that, the trap was set, and the hunter had no idea he'd just invited his own ruin.

* * *

The Encounter…

The night air hung thick over the lake, humid and heavy with secrets. A veil of mist curled across the dark water, blurring the line between sky and reflection. Thalía moved down the narrow dock, her heels tapping softly against the wood, each step steady, deliberate.

Mayor Finley was already there, swaying slightly, glass of whiskey in hand, his confidence as inflated as his ego. He grinned when he saw her, teeth flashing beneath the low light of the dock lamp.

"Hi, Sandra, you made it," he slurred, extending a hand. "My name… ah, never mind. Doesn't matter anyway. Let's have some fun!"

Thalía took his hand, her touch light, her smile practiced. Inside, disgust twisted like barbed wire, but she hid it behind a soft laugh. "Of course," she purred. "Let's."

The boat rocked gently as she stepped aboard, the sound of her heels echoing like a countdown. Inside the cabin, the air was close and warm, thick with cologne and cheap liquor. Finley poured two drinks with shaky precision, spilling whiskey across the counter. He started to talk; bragging, boasting about his power, his protection, how he owned this town, how no one could touch him.

Thalía listened, nodding, her lips curling in quiet amusement. Every word he spoke only confirmed what she already knew: this man believed he was invincible.

And that made her job easier.

They set out onto the lake, the city lights shrinking until nothing remained but darkness and the hum of the motor. When Finley finally cut the engine, silence swallowed them whole. The water lapped softly against the hull—steady, patient, waiting.

Finley stumbled toward her, his grin sloppy, his eyes glazed. "C'mere, sweetheart," he muttered, reaching for her waist.

Thalía didn't move at first. She simply watched him—the way power made him pathetic, the way lust made him blind. Then, with a faint smile, she let him pull her close.

Two more drinks in, and he was on her—clumsy hands, heavy breath, the reek of entitlement. Thalía didn't resist, she let it happen. She let him have his way with her; She knew what she had come here to do., every gesture controlled, every sound deliberate.

It was quick. Careless. Exactly what she expected.

And when it was done, she stared past him, through the cabin window, at the dark expanse of water stretching endlessly into the night.

Because this—this was the calm before the storm.

* * *

The Aftermath…

Afterward, as Mayor Finley lay sprawled across the bed—smug, spent, and utterly defenseless. Thalía moved with quiet precision. From her purse, she retrieved a small glass vial, the same one she had slipped into his second drink. The sedative was potent; within minutes, his breath slowed, his limbs heavy, his arrogance dissolved into a deep, dreamless sleep.

Thalía stood over him for a long moment, watching his chest rise and fall. Disgust twisted in her gut—not just for what he'd done, but for the ease with which men like him believed they could take whatever they wanted.

Then, turning away, she stepped into the bathroom. The mirror glared back at her beneath the sterile light. She reached into her purse again, pulled out a tube of thick red lipstick, and leaned close to the glass.

With slow, deliberate strokes, she wrote:

'Welcome to the disease that there is no cure for!'

The message bled crimson across the mirror, the words jagged, angry, final.

Without another glance, Thalía slipped back into her dress, gathered her purse, and left the boat cabin. The night air hit her skin like freedom. Quietly, she lowered the emergency dinghy into the lake, climbed aboard, and rowed away, leaving the mayor's boat to drift silently on the black, endless water.

By the time she reached the shore, the eastern sky had begun to pale. She stepped onto the dock, calm and composed, her heels clicking softly against the wood. Thalía slipped her hand into her purse, retrieved her phone and the folded flyer from the charity event, the one she'd kept for this very reason—her final link to the mayor's world, and sent a message to Finley's wife.

Her fingers moved steadily across the screen.

Do not be intimate with your husband again. He's carrying something that has no cure, and very contagious. You've been warned.

She stared at the message for a moment, then pressed *send*.

Somewhere out on the lake, a powerful man slept, oblivious to the storm that was about to consume his perfect world.

Another monster marked.

Another secret unearthed.

And Thalía was far from finished.

CHAPTER 62

The Reckoning

Mayor Finley's head felt like it was splitting in two pieces when he finally came to. The pounding in his skull matched the dizzying churn of the boat beneath him. He groaned, pushing himself upright, every movement dragging through the haze of disorientation.

He had no idea how long he'd been out. The last thing he remembered was being with Sandra—her perfume, her laughter, and then… nothing. Just a blur, the kind of blackout that only alcohol or something stronger could cause.

He rubbed his temples, blinking hard. The sheets were rumpled. The air smelled of sex, sweat, and regret. His body felt heavy, too comfortable, too exposed—and somewhere deep inside, a flicker of unease began to grow.

Unsteady on his feet, he stumbled toward the bathroom and flicked on the light.

That's when he saw it.

Scrawled across the mirror in thick red lipstick were the words:

'Welcome to the disease that there is no cure for!'

His breath hitched. The message stared back at him like a wound, burning into his reflection.

At first, he thought it was some kind of sick joke. But then, like ice water down his spine, the memory came rushing back, the case files. The reports. Two other men, each found with the same cryptic message after anonymous encounters. Both later diagnosed with HIV.

Finley's heart began to race. The blood drained from his face.

There was no mistaking it.

He was one of them now.

A sick panic clawed up his throat as he gripped the edge of the sink, his knuckles whitening. Images flashed through his mind, every woman he'd cheated with, every lie he'd told, every abuse of power he thought he'd gotten away with. It all came flooding back, and with it, the realization that karma had finally caught him.

His chest tightened. His reflection blurred through the sting of sweat and fear.

He staggered back into the cabin just as his phone began to buzz. On the screen: **Wifee**.

He hesitated, then answered. Her voice trembled through the receiver.

"Richard, where have you been? I've been calling all night. I just got a message from an unknown number. It said, 'Do not sleep with your husband again. He's carrying something that has no cure. You've been warned.'

"The message was sent to the government phone, in which you know are closely monitored. This is now going to be public information"!

What does that mean? Are you okay?"

Finley froze. Her words cut through him like glass. His throat went dry; he couldn't form a response. The truth hovered at the edges of his mind—ugly, undeniable, irreversible.

He sank into a chair, phone still pressed to his ear, his heart pounding like a drum of guilt and dread. Sandra, if that was even her real name, had done this. She had played him. Exposed him.

And now his perfect world; his wife, his position, his power— was unraveling faster than he could breathe.

As he sat there, staring into the empty space where she had been, a single realization hit him harder than the hangover ever could:

He wasn't the predator anymore.

He was the prey.

And there would be no escape.

CHAPTER 63

The Fall

By the time Miami woke the next morning, the city was already in chaos. Headlines screamed from every newsstand and TV screen:

"Mayor Finley Under Investigation: Anonymous Accusations Rock City Hall"

"Scandal Hits City's Top Office: Secrets, Lies, and a Mysterious Woman"

"Is Finley's Empire of Power Crumbling?"

The media had erupted into a frenzy. Every post, every headline dissected every angle, every rumor, every scandalous possibility. The mayor's carefully curated image of control and sophistication was shattered, replaced by whispers of betrayal, disease, and corruption.

Inside the mayoral mansion, the tension was palpable. Mrs. Finley stood in the kitchen, phone in hand, eyes wide and trembling as she scrolled through the incoming messages. Every news alert, every forwarded text, painted a picture she had refused to accept: her husband, unfaithful, exposed, and now carrying a deadly secret.

"Richard!" she demanded, voice cracking as she spun toward him, her hands shaking. "What is going on? Who sent me this message? What... what have you done?"

Mayor Finley, still reeling from his night of terror and shame, could only stare at her. The panic in his own chest mirrored the fear in hers. For the first time in decades, he was powerless, stripped of control, completely vulnerable.

"I... I don't know," he stammered, his voice weak, unconvincing. "It... it's nothing. Just a... a mistake."

"A mistake?" she spat, disbelief and anger mingling. "Do you realize what this means? Everyone knows. The press, the city, your staff... even your friends! You've humiliated yourself and our entire family"

Her hands trembled as her eyes locked into her husband's with a sharp, cold intensity. "You know what?" she said, her voice steady but dripping with fury. "I've known about your affairs for years. I endured it for the sake of this family, for your career, for appearances. I have humiliated myself time and time again in front of my friends and colleagues, as most all of them already knew. But now I'm done, Richard. I'm done. I want a divorce. And this time, I won't stay silent."

Her voice faltered as the magnitude of the betrayal, the disease, the lies sank in. Finley opened his mouth to interrupt, to justify, but no words could patch the fissure she had just witnessed.

Outside, the city buzzed with speculation. Council members whispered in corridors, reporters called incessantly, and political opponents smelled blood in the water. The mayor's schedule, once packed with meetings and photo ops, now lay in ruins. Invitations were rescinded. Public appearances canceled. Every ounce of authority he had clung to for decades teetered on the edge of collapse.

And somewhere in the city, Thalía watched it all unfold from a distance, calm, composed, invisible. Another monster marked. Another empire crumbling under the weight of its own arrogance.

She didn't celebrate. She simply noted the precision of her work, the inevitability of consequences finally catching up with those who thought themselves untouchable.

Her phone buzzed lightly in her hand. Another name. Another target.

And the hunt continued.

CHAPTER 64

Concord of Ashes

Weeks slid by and Thalía remained unseen. She kept her head low, stalking the city in quiet, patient silence, waiting for the exact face she wanted to hand a fate she'd already decided. Her hunt was surgical; this wasn't about random cruelty. It was about choosing the right targets and delivering a punishment that fit.

Meanwhile, the city's two newest pariahs were learning how quickly a private hell could become public. Tony and Mayor Finley had both tested positive for HIV. Panic, shame, and fury replaced the arrogance that had once defined them. Tony raged like a cornered animal, vowing to find Thalía and end her. Finley's life unraveled: his wife left, divorce papers were filed, and his political shield dissolved into chatter and contempt. He, too, swore revenge.

None of that mattered if they couldn't find her.

The rain whispered against the cold concrete of an abandoned parking garage as night settled. Pools of water shimmered beneath the sodium lamps, mirroring two lives fractured by the same impossible secret. Tony leaned against his black Cadillac, the engine ticking like an angry beast cooling down. He lit a cigarette with hands that trembled, the smoke a thin, futile shield. His velvet jacket, darkened at the shoulders, clung to him like an accusation.

From the shadows, a figure emerged in a rain-darkened trench coat, Mayor Finley. The city's golden mayor now looked smaller somehow, his tailored suit sagging under exhaustion and disgrace. His eyes, once sharp, were hollow, the brightness of his public persona extinguished.

They regarded one another across the wet floor. For a long beat there were no words, just a tension thicker than the storm overhead.

"Well, well," Tony grated, flicking ash carelessly. "Look who finally slithered out from behind his golden desk."

Finley did not flinch. His voice came low, flat. "Save it, Tony. I'm not here for small talk."

Tony pushed off the car and closed the distance slowly. "Let's talk real-talk, Finley. Word is… you caught what I caught."

Finley said nothing, he didn't need to. The silence spoke for both of them. When he finally answered it came with a bitter half-smile. Tony barked the words no one wanted to hear again: "Did she leave you that same fucked-up message? WELCOME TO THE DISEASE THAT THERE IS NO CURE FOR? That shit will be etched in my head for as long as I live."

The mayor said (jokingly), well according to the Docs, that won't be long for either one of us now will it, and chuckled it off. But the joke fell flat. It was everything neither of them wanted to face. "Accept it, Tony. There's no cure in sight. Laugh it off while you can."

"Fuck you," Tony snapped. "This isn't a joke."

"She did this," Finley said quietly. "Thalía."

Tony's laugh was dry and humorless. "Damn right she did. Girl's got poison in her smile. Used me like a syringe, spread the sickness knowing full well what she was doing."

Finley's lips drew tight. "She played us both. And now, my wife's gone. Filed for divorce. My name's in every headline like some disease." Anger and humiliation twisted together until they were indistinguishable.

Tony's stare went cold. "I should've known better. But you? Mr. Clean-Cut Mayor? You should've been smarter."

"Don't preach," Finley said. "We're in the same grave now."

Rain pelted the roof. Once allies in the city's underbelly, trading favors and whispered compromises, they were now linked by something far darker. The truth burned louder than thunder.

"She's disappeared," Tony muttered. "I've torn the streets up, strips, motels, underground spots. Nothing. It's like she vanished."

"She hasn't," Finley replied. "She's still out there. Watching. Waiting. She's not hiding. She's hunting."

Tony crushed his cigarette beneath his boot. "Then maybe it's time we hunt her."

Finley's eyes narrowed. "You suggesting we work together, again?"

Tony nodded. "Like the old days. No politics. No rules. Just vengeance."

A slow, dangerous smile creased Finley's worn face. "Justice."

"Revenge," Tony corrected.

The pact was sealed in that wet, fluorescent-soured air: two broken men with nothing left to lose, setting out to reclaim what they thought was theirs. They walked away together into the rain, a makeshift alliance forged in fear and fury.

Unbeknownst to them, hidden high in the shadows of a rooftop, a figure watched and listened to every word, every plan.

It was Thalía. Calm, composed, and utterly in control, she observed with the patience of a predator who already knew the terrain. A faint, knowing smile touched her lips. They moved exactly as she had predicted—reckless, desperate, predictable. She tucked her hands beneath her coat, melted back into the darkness, and disappeared into the city's pulse. The hunt would continue, and she was already two steps ahead.

Chapter 65

The Search is On

By the next day, Mayor Finley's rage had reached a fever pitch. Humiliation, fear, and disease had driven him to a singular obsession: finding Thalía. He envisioned her captured, broken, and paying for the chaos she had unleashed on his life. Every waking thought revolved around her, where she could be, how he could get to her, and how he could make her suffer.

Tony and his network of thugs became extensions of the mayor's fury. "Scour the streets. Clubs. Motels. Underground scenes. Every alley, every corner," Finley barked over the phone, his voice tight with anger. "When you find her, save her for me. Don't touch her, don't kill her, bring her to me. I want her, alive or dead, but alive first."

The city became a hunting ground. Tony's men fanned out, leaving no stone unturned, interrogating bartenders, security guards, and street hustlers. Finley leveraged every contact, every political favor, every officer loyal to him. Nothing was too small; nothing too trivial.

Then came the media assault. Finley made a series of frantic calls, forcing news stations to broadcast her mugshot, plaster her image across the internet, and publicize a reward, a bounty for anyone who could locate the woman who had shattered his empire.

"Murder," the headlines screamed. "Dangerous fugitive. Approach with caution."

Within hours, Thalía became more than a ghost—she was a target, a lightning rod of fear and obsession for two of the city's most dangerous men. The story spread beyond Miami, into neighboring states, and even into international news channels, painting her as a criminal mastermind with a deadly secret. Governments and law enforcement offices quietly circulated her picture in intelligence networks, just in case she had fled abroad.

Thalía felt the shift immediately. The city she had moved through unnoticed for weeks now felt like a trap. Every cab, every flicker of neon, every passerby could be a potential threat. She had to change her patterns, avoid familiar streets, and be more unpredictable than ever. Even her briefest outings required careful planning, timing, and contingencies.

She moved like a shadow, quiet and deliberate, blending into the crowds she had once observed with ease. Her instincts sharpened. She became hyper-aware of every reflection in glass, every footstep behind her, every glance from strangers.

The stakes had never been higher. Every step forward was calculated. Every move, a measure of survival. And while the city hunted her, she hunted her own space—her freedom, her safety, and the inevitable moment when she would turn the tables once again.

CHAPTER 66

Bloodlines

Marco...

Marco had just returned home from his fútbol game, kicked off his cleats and stepped into the house. Still buzzing from the game as he'd scored the winning goal, the kind of moment that made the whole town shout, and he rode the afterglow all the way to his front door. Eleanor waited there, face drawn and serious; the light from the hallway made her features look sharp.

"Have you seen the news?" she asked before he could set his bag down.

"No," Marco said, shrugging, a proud grin breaking through. "I've been busy, we won! I scored the winning goal—yesss!" He held up his hand as if the memory could still be touched.

"That's great, sweetheart," Eleanor said, forcing a smile that didn't reach her eyes. "But come with me. Now!"

"Can I at least shower first?" he asked, wiping grass from his socks.

"No shower," she replied, gently but firmly. "Just put your bag down and come with me. I have a surprise."

His grin flickered into a worried smile. "Okay... I like surprises, I guess."

She took his hand and practically led him into the living room. The TV was already on; the news crawl scrolled like a river of bad tidings. Eleanor didn't speak, she only pointed.

Marco stared at the screen. Then the image hit him like a physical blow: a mugshot, stark and unforgiving. The chyron labeled her a wanted fugitive, dangerous, but he didn't see that. His eyes locked on the face, tracing the lines as if he could redraw the past. The stranger on the screen was older than the girl he remembered— harder—but the eyes were the same: mismatched eye color (heterochromia).

A bolt of recognition tore through him. He went still, breath caught in his throat. Tears sprang unbidden and hot behind his lids.

"That's her," he said, voice breaking. "That's Thalía." He turned to Eleanor, nearly shaking. "That's my cousin! Look, her eyes. It's Thalía. Oh my God, I can't believe we've found her!"

Overwhelmed, he kissed Eleanor on the cheek and grabbed her shoulders, wild with urgency.

"Where is she? Where is she? Let's go get her right now!"

Eleanor held him tightly, trying to steady him.

"Marco," she said gently, "I know how excited you are. I'm excited too, but you need to sit down. Listen to what they're saying about her first."

Reluctantly, Marco sat beside her, wiping his tears as the television continued airing footage and commentary. News anchors spoke in grave tones, words like 21 year old female, *dangerous* and *wanted* echoing in his ears. Charges. Sightings. Deaths.

He turned to Eleanor slowly, disbelief etched across his face.

"No... No, this can't be my cousin," he whispered. "She's a good girl. She's not a murderer. *They're lying.* I know her, Eleanor. She wouldn't hurt anyone!"

Marco's hands trembled as he clutched Eleanor's arm. "We need to get on the first plane over there, bring her home. Where she belongs!"

Eleanor's expression darkened. She took his hands in hers, steady but firm.

"Marco," she said quietly, "you have to understand. She's a wanted fugitive right now. There's no way they'll let her board a plane. The moment she shows up at an airport, they'll arrest her, maybe worse."

His eyes searched hers, desperation giving way to dawning realization. Slowly, he nodded, swallowing hard as the truth sank in.

"You're right," he murmured. "You're right..."

The two sat in silence for a moment, the weight of the situation settling between them.

Then, as if sparked by the same thought, their eyes met again—no longer in shock, but in determination. Fear tempered into strategy, they began to speak in quieter tones:

They didn't say it aloud, but the wheels had begun to turn.

If Thalía couldn't come home the normal way, they'd have to find another.

Somehow… some way… they would get her out.

Back to Honduras.

Back to family.

Back to safety.

Poor Little Poor Girl

CHAPTER 67

Discovering Routes

The silence didn't last long.

Marco rose and began to pace, every step a metronome for a mind racing too fast to rest. Eleanor watched him quietly—patient, steady, knowing better than to interrupt the storm as it gathered.

"We can't go through airports," he said, more to himself than to her. "They'll be watching those like hawks. Passports, scanners, facial recognition, everything's a trap."

Eleanor nodded. "We need something under the radar. Something quiet."

A light clicked on in Marco's eyes. He snapped his fingers. "Boats. Small commuter planes. Cargo ships. People slip through ports all the time, no one notices a crate or a deckhand."

"You want to smuggle her onto a ship?" Eleanor asked, skeptical but curious.

"Not ideal," he admitted, thinking as he spoke, "but doable. Or private transport, someone who doesn't ask questions. We just need the right contact."

Eleanor chewed her lower lip, then offered the name she'd been turning over. "My former client, Javier. He works on the docks over in Havana, Cuba. He owes me, big time. He knows the smaller family-run vessels, the kinds that don't show up on radar lists. If we can get her there…"

Marco finished the thought. "Havana is a perfect waypoint. From there you can fly into Honduras with less fuss. If we can get her to Havana, the rest becomes a real route."

"And I have another avenue," Eleanor added. "An American friend from years back, Fort Lauderdale. He knows people who arrange private flights. Quiet planes, private manifests. If he can hook us up, we could move her north to Havana without touching customs."

Marco's face shifted from worry to focus. "Yes. That's it. Havana's our bridge. We get her there, we get her home."

"But first," Eleanor said gently, grounding him, "we have to find her. And we have to find her before someone else does."

The room swallowed the truth like a weight. Marco's shoulders tightened; the urgency settled back in.

"I'll call my connect tonight," he said. "He's got people in Miami. Someone might have seen her, maybe she's laying low where she used to move, someplace familiar."

"And I'll call Javier," Eleanor replied. "Quietly. No messages on traceable phones. If we can set up a route in advance, we give her a place to disappear into, no paperwork, no questions."

They met each other's gaze, no longer shocked, no longer pleading, but resolved. Loyalty braided with practicality. Fear tempered into planning.

Whatever had happened, whatever the headlines screamed, Marco would not abandon his blood. They would find her and bring her home.

No matter what it took.

CHAPTER 68

The Hunter's Call

Thalía…

Thalía felt it before it happened.

The room had gone too quiet—too still, as if the night itself were holding its breath. She stood by the window, watching the glow of the big city bleed across the glass, when her phone vibrated in her palm.

No number.

No name.

Just *Unknown*.

Her pulse stuttered.

She answered anyway.

For a moment, there was only static—low, deliberate, like someone breathing on the other end. Then a voice slid through the silence, smooth and venomous, carrying an accent she knew in her bones.

"Did you think you vanished?" Hamza said softly. "Did you really believe that I would forget what belongs to me?" "I'm too rich for that", he said.

Her grip tightened until her knuckles burned.

"I found you," he continued, almost amused. "You were careful. I'll give you that. New shadows. New names. New lies." A pause. A smile she could hear. "But blood leaves a trail."

"And with the help of my good friend Mr. Mayor Finley, we finally tracked you down," Hamza said, his tone thick with satisfaction.

Thalía's chest seized.

Hamza says, listen to this someone wants to tell you something.

Thalía immediately gets extremely nervous thinking, maybe they have kidnapped Cheney, Cynthia, or someone innocent that she actually cares about, as hostage in exchange for her.

Panic surged as she braced herself to surrender everything she had left if it meant sparing them.

She was ready to say, "I'll come, *I'll give myself up. Just let them go.*"

But before the words could leave her mouth, another voice cut through the line—grating, smug, unmistakably cruel.

"Well howdy there pretty lady"!

Her stomach dropped.

It was Mayor Finley.

Then she hears Tony in the background yelling, "Aye, aye, tell that bitch I said what's up". While laughing he says, we found you and coming to get you, payback's a BITCH! Ha ha ha!

In that instant, the final piece snapped into place.

They were all connected—Hamza, Finley, Tony—threads of the same rotten web. A trafficking ring disguised by corrupt politics, money, and influence, exploiting power to stay untouchable.

Fear coursed through Thalía—but beneath it, a sharp, unexpected relief.

They hadn't found her friends.

They hadn't used them to reach her.

This hunt was for *her* alone.

And now she knew exactly who she was up against.

Outside, a car rolled past—slow. Too slow.

"You're hunting ghosts," Thalía said, forcing steel into her voice. "I'm not your property."

A chuckle. Cold. Certain.

"You always were," Hamza replied. "And I am coming to collect."

Thalía became paranoid; her window flared with headlights. Once. Then again, closer.

"My men are already moving," he said. "Check your street. Count the exits. Decide who you'll trust." Another pause, sharpened to a blade. "Run if you want. It will only make the ending sweeter."

The line went dead.

She thought, she'd been found.

Thalía backed away from the window as a knock sounded—soft, patient, inevitable.

The hunt for her was in full-force!

To Be Continued. . . .

Stay tuned—what remains unfinished will be answered in Part Two, the final book of the series, coming in Spring 2026!

Author's Note

This part of the story ends, but the realities that inspired it does not.

While Thalía Salazar's journey is a work of fiction, it is rooted in truths lived by countless individuals whose stories are rarely told, believed, or given justice. Human trafficking, exploitation, and systemic failure are not distant horrors—they exist in our communities, our institutions, and our silences.

This book was written with care, responsibility, and respect for those whose lives echo aspects of this narrative. It does not claim to represent every experience, nor could it. No single story ever can. But it was written in the belief that storytelling has power: to confront denial, to foster empathy, and to challenge the comfort of looking away.

If this book unsettled you, that discomfort has purpose. If it moved you, let that movement continue beyond the final page. Awareness alone is not enough—listening, believing, and acting matter.

To survivors: your courage is real, your pain is not forgotten, and your voice matters, even when it feels unheard.

To readers: thank you for bearing witness.

May this story remain not only something you read, but something you carry forward, with compassion, vigilance, and the resolve to stand against injustice wherever it is found.

Please post a Review for 'Poor Little Poor Girl' Books 1 and 2 at the links below:

- ➤ Poor Little Poor Girl - Book 1: https://books2read.com/PLPG1

- ➤ Poor Little Poor Girl - Book 2: https://books2read.com/PLPG2

- ➤ https://www.wynningentertainment.com/poor-little-poor-girl-feedback

Information for *Poor Little Poor Girl - Book 2* below:

ISBNs:

Paperback: 979-8-9942005-2-0 // Hardcover: 979-8-1986000-3-4

eBook: 979-8-9942005-3-7 // Audiobook: 979-8-9942005-5-1

Social Media:

Website: www.wynningentertainment.com/home

Instagram: https://www.instagram.com/wynning_entertainment/ or wynningwithlink

YouTube: https://www.youtube.com/channel/UC6Z8yRE2yOdyMKOFCW0c3eg

TikTok: https://www.tiktok.com/@wynningent

Facebook: https://www.facebook.com/link.linc.1